This edition will make widely available for the first time a suppressed novel by a famous American playwright. Printed in a limited edition of two thousand copies in 1922 and privately circulated, it was confiscated by the Federal Government as obscene.

A novel of decadence in the tradition of Against Nature *by Huysmans,* Fantazius Mallare *is the story of a mad recluse—a gifted sculptor and painter—who is at war with reality. Watching his genius die, Mallare retreats into a world of hallucination, which becomes more real than life itself. He believes he should have been a God. To achieve omnipotence he must have a woman. He finds Rita, a submissive gypsy girl, whom he struggles to possess without "the loathesome absurdities of sex."*

MALLARE

FANTAZIUS
MALLARE

A Mysterious Oath

BEN HECHT

Drawings
WALLACE SMITH

A Harvest/HBJ Book
Harcourt Brace Jovanovich
New York and London

Library of Congress Cataloging in Publication Data

Hecht, Ben, 1893–1964.
Fantazius Mallare.

(A Harvest/HBJ book)
Reprint of the ed. published by Covici-McGee, Chicago.
I. Title.
[PZ3.H355Fan   1978]   [PS3515.E18]   813'.5'2   78-6637
ISBN 0-15-630160-1

First Harvest/HBJ edition 1978

A B C D E F G H I J

Drawings

&

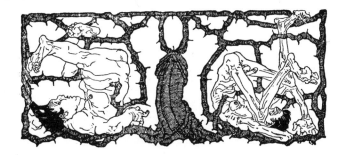

DEDICATION

HIS dark and wayward book is affectionately dedicated to my enemies—to the curious ones who take fanatic pride in disliking me; to the baffling ones who remain enthusiastically ignorant of my existence; to the moral ones upon whom Beauty exercises a lascivious and corrupting influence; to the moral ones who have relentlessly chased God out of their bedrooms; to the moral ones who cringe before Nature, who flatten themselves upon prayer rugs, who shut their eyes, stuff their ears, bind, gag and truss themselves and offer their mutilations to the idiot God they

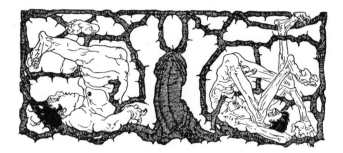

have invented (*the Devil take them, I grow
bored with laughing at them*); to the anointed
ones who identify their paranoic symptoms as
virtues, who build altars upon complexes; to
the anointed ones who have slain themselves and
who stagger proudly into graves (*God deliver
Himself from their caress!*); to the religious
ones who wage bloody and tireless wars upon
all who do not share their fear of life (*Ah,
what is God but a despairing refutation of
Man?*); to the solemn and successful ones who
gesture with courteous disdain from the depth
of their ornamental coffins (*we are all cadavers
but let us refrain from congratulating each
other too courteously on the fact*); to the prim
ones who find their secret obscenities mirrored in every careless phrase, who read self
accusation into the word sex; to the prim ones
who wince adroitly in the hope of being mis-
taken for imbeciles; to the prim ones who

fornicate apologetically (the Devil can-cans in their souls); to the cowardly ones who borrow their courage from Ideals which they forthwith defend with their useless lives; to the cowardly ones who adorn themselves with castrations (let this not be misunderstood); to the reformers—the psychopathic ones who publicly and shamelessly belabor their own unfortunate impulses; to the reformers (once again)—the psychopathic ones trying forever to drown their own obscene desires in ear-splitting prayers for their fellowman's welfare; to the reformers— the Freudian dervishes who masturbate with Purity Leagues, who achieve involved orgasms denouncing the depravities of others; to the reformers (patience, patience) the psychopathic ones who seek to vindicate their own sexual impotencies by padlocking the national vagina, who find relief for constipation in forbidding their neighbors the water closet (God forgives

them, *but not I*); to the ostracizing ones who hurl excommunications upon all that is not part of their stupidity; to the ostracizing ones who fraternize only with the worms inside their coffins (their anger is the caress incomparable); to the pious ones who, lacking the strength to please themselves, boast interminably to God of their weakness in denying themselves; to the idealistic ones who, unable to confound their neighbors with their own superiority, join causes in the hope of confounding each other with the superiority of their betters (involved, but I am not done with them); to the idealistic ones whose cowardice converts the suffering of others into a mirror wherein stares wretchedly back at them a possible image of themselves; to the idealistic ones who, frightened by this possible image of themselves, join Movements for the triumph of Love and Justice and the overthrow of Tyranny in the frantic hope of break-

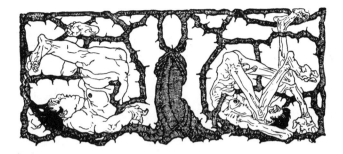

ing the mirror; to the social ones who regard belching as the sin against the Holy Ghost, who enamel themselves with banalities, who repudiate contemptuously the existence of their bowels (*Ah, these theologians of etiquette, these unctuous circumlocutors, a pock upon them*); to the pure ones who masquerade excitedly as eunuchs and as wives of eunuchs (*they have their excuses, of course, and who knows but the masquerade is somewhat unnecessary*); to the pedantic ones who barricade themselves heroically behind their own belchings; to the smug ones who walk with their noses ecstatically buried in their own rectums (*I have nothing against them, I swear*); to the righteous ones who masturbate blissfully under the blankets of their perfections; to the righteous ones who finger each other in the choir loft (*God forgive me if I ever succumb to one of them*); to the critical ones who whoremonger on Parnassus; to the

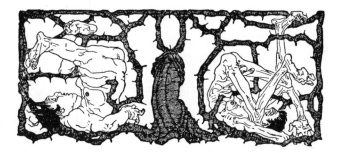

critical ones who befoul themselves in the Temples and point embitteredly at the Gods as the sources of their own odors (*I will someday devote an entire dedication to critics*); to the proud ones who urinate against the wind (*they have never wetted me and I have nothing against them*); to the cheerful ones who tirade viciously against all who do not wear their protective smirk; to the cheerful ones who spend their evenings bewailing my existence (*the Devil pity them, not I*); to the noble ones who advertise their secrets, who crucify themselves on billboards in the quest for the Nietzschean solitude; to the noble ones who pride themselves on their stolen finery; to the flagellating ones who go to the opera in hair shirts, who excite themselves with denials and who fornicate only on Fast Days; to the just ones who find compensation for their nose rings and sackcloth by hamstringing all who refuse to put them on

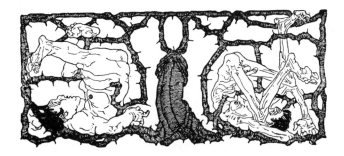

—all who have committed the alluring sins from which their own cowardice fled; to the conservative ones who gnaw elatedly upon old bones and wither with malnutrition; to the conservative ones who snarl, yelp, whimper and grunt, who are the parasites of death; who choke themselves with their beards; to the timorous ones who vomit invective upon all that confuses them, who vituperate against all their non-existent intelligence cannot grasp; to the martyr ones who disembowel themselves on the battlefield, who crucify themselves upon their stupidities; to the serious ones who mistake the sleep of their senses and the snores of their intellect for enviable perfections; to the serious ones who suffocate gently in the boredom they create (God alone has time to laugh at them); to the virgin ones who tenaciously advertise their predicament; to the virgin ones who mourn themselves, who kneel before key-

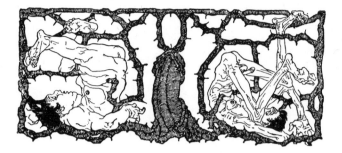

*holes; to the holy ones who recommend them-
selves tirelessly and triumphantly to God (I
have never envied God His friends, nor He,
mine perhaps); to the never clean ones who
bathe publicly in the hysterias of the mob; to
the never clean ones who pander for stupidity;
to the intellectual ones who play solitaire with
platitudes, who drag their classrooms around
with them; to these and to many other abominations whom I apologize to for omitting, this
inhospitable book, celebrating the dark mirth
of Fantazius Mallare, is dedicated in the hope
that their righteous eyes may never kindle with
secret lusts nor their pious lips water erotically
from its reading—in short in the hope that
they may never encounter the ornamental
phrases I have written and the ritualistic lines
Wallace Smith has drawn in the pages that
follow.*

MALLARE

WALLACE
SMITH

{I}

ANTAZIUS MALLARE considered himself mad because he was unable to behold in the meaningless gesturings of time, space and evolution a dramatic little pantomime adroitly centered about the routine of his existence. He was a silent looking man with black hair and an aquiline nose. His eyes were lifeless because they paid no homage to the world outside him.

When he was thirty-five years old he lived alone high above a busy part of the town. He was a recluse. His black hair that fell in a slant across his forehead and the rigidity of his eyes gave him the appearance of a somnam-

bulist. He found life unnecessary and sub-
mitted to it without curiosity.

His ideas were profoundly simple. The
excitement of his neighborhood, his city, his
country and his world left him unmoved. He
found no diversion in interpreting them. A
friend had once asked him what he thought
of democracy. This was during a great war
being waged in its behalf. Mallare replied:
"Democracy is the honeymoon of stupidity."

There lived with him as a servant a little
monster whom he called Goliath and who was
a dwarfed and paralytic negro. Goliath's age
was unknown. His deformities gave him the
air of an old man and his hunched back made
him seem too massive for a boy. But in studying him Mallare had concluded that he was
a boy.

Goliath had been one of the first symptoms
of Mallare's madness. He had brought the little
monster home from an amusement park one
summer night. Goliath had been s t a n d i n g
doubled up, his pipe stem arms hanging like a

baboon's, his enlarged black head lifted and his furious eyes staring at a Wheel of Fortune.

When they left the confetti-electrics of the park behind, Mallare spoke to the dwarf whose wrinkled hand he was holding.

"If you come home with me I will make you a servant and give you a fine red suit to wear. Also, I will call you Goliath for no reason at all, since I am at war with reason."

Goliath said nothing but sat staring happily out of the window of an automobile as they rode home.

The home of Fantazius Mallare was filled with evidences of his past. There were clay and bronze figures and canvases covered with paintings. These had been the work of his hands. It was to be seen that he had once given himself with violence to the creation of images. And for this reason he was still known among a few people as an artist.

In the days when he had worked to create images Mallare had been alive with derisions.

He desired to give them outline. But the desire went from him. The brilliant fancies of his thought began slowly to bore him. The astounding images that still bowed themselves into his mind became like a procession of mendicants seeking alms of him. He folded his hands and with an interested smile watched his genius die.

At the time of this curious tragedy Mallare was thirty. He kept a Journal in which he wrote infrequently. There was in this Journal little of interest. Apparently he had amused himself during his youth jotting down items of preposterous unimportance.

"I saw a man with a red face," he would write one week. The next he would add a line, "There are seven hundred and eighty-five normal strides between the lamp-post and my front door." Turning a page a month later he would meticulously set down the date, the hour of the day, the direction of the wind and under it write out, "I have a stomach ache from eating peaches."

The Journal bristled with innocuous informations. An acquaintance of the period, interested in Mallare's work as an artist, smiled and commented, "These are, no doubt, symbols. A psychological code into which you have translated great inner moments."

Mallare answered, "On the contrary. They are the only thoughts I have had in which I could detect no reason. It has amused me to put down with great care the few banalities which have normalized my days. They are very precious to me, although they have no value in themselves.

"It is the ability to think such absurdities as you have read that has kept me from suicide. The will to live is no more than the hypnotism of banalities. We keep alive only by maintaining, despite our intelligence, an enthusiasm for things which are of no consequence or interest to us.

"That I saw a man with a red face aroused in me a gentle curiosity lacking in words or emotion. The desire to live is compounded of an infinity of such gentle curiosities which remain entirely outside of reason. This never-satisfied and almost non-existent curiosity we have toward things, masquerades under the intimidating guise of the law of self-preservation. Man is at the mercy of life since, his intelligence perceiving its monotony and absurdity, he still clings to it, fascinated by the accumulated rhythm of faces, impressions, and events which he despises.

"It is a form of hypnosis, and these words I have written in my Journal are the absurdities by which life seduced me from abandoning it. I am grateful to them and have therefore preserved them carefully."

The history of Mallare's madness, however, is to be found in this Journal. There are two empty pages that stare significantly. The empty pages are a lapse. It was during this lapse that Mallare smiled with interest at the spectacle of his disintegration. There follows, then, a sudden excited outburst, undated. In it the beginnings of his madness pirouette like tentative dancers.

"Perhaps the greatest miracle is that which enables man to tolerate life," the passage starts, "which enables him to embrace its illusions and translate its monstrous incoherence into delightful, edifying patterns. It is the miracle of sanity. To stand unquestioning before mysteries, to remain an undisturbed part of chaos, ah! what an adjustment! Content and even elate amid the terrible circle of Unknowns, behold in this the heroic stupidity of the sane. . . a stupidity which has already outlived the Gods.

"Man, alas, is the only animal who hasn't known enough to die. His undeveloped senses have permitted him to survive in the manner of the oyster. The mysteries, dangers, and delights of the sea do not exist for the oyster. Its senses are not stirred by typhoons, impressed by earthquakes or annoyed by its own insignificance. Similarly, man!

"The complacent egomania of man, his tyrannical indifferences, his little list of questions and answers which suffices for his wisdom, these are the chief phenomena or symptoms of his sanity. He alone has survived the ages by means of a series of ludicrous adjustments, until today he walks on two legs—the crowning absurdity of an otherwise logical Nature. He has triumphed by specializing in his weaknesses and insuring their survival; by disputing the simple laws of biology with interminable banalities labelled from age to age as religions, philosophies and laws.

"Unable, despite his shiftiness, to lie the the fact of his mortality and decomposition out of existence, he has satisfied his mania for survival by the invention of souls. And so behold him—spectacle of spectacles—a chatty little tradesman in an immemorial hat drifting good-naturedly through a nightmare.

"It is for this ability to exist unnaturally that he has invented the adjective sane. But here and there in the streets of cities walk the damned—creatures denied the miracle of sanity and who move bewilderedly through their scene, staring at the flying days as at the fragments of another world. They are conscious of themselves only as vacuums within which life is continually expiring.

"Alas, the damned! From the depths of their non-existence they contemplate their fellowman and perceive him a dwarf prostrate forever before solacing arrangements of words; an homunculus riding vaingloriously on the tiny river of ink that flows between monstrous yesterdays and monstrous tomorrows; a baboon strutting through a mirage."

The history of Mallare's madness begins thus. And the pages continue. The writing on them seems at a glance part of a decoration in black and white. The letters are beautifully formed and shaded. They resemble laboring serpents, dainty pagodas, vines bearing strange fruits and capricious bits of sculpture.

To the end Mallare fancied himself aware of the drift and nuance of his madness. Its convolutions seemed neither incomprehensible nor mysterious to him.

An intolerable loathing for life, an illuminated contempt for men and women, had long ago taken possession of him. This philosophic attitude was the product of his egoism. He felt himself the center of life and it became his nature to revolt against all evidences of life that existed outside himself. In this manner he grew to hate, or rather to feel an impotent disgust for, whatever was contemporary.

When his normality abandoned him, he avoided a greater tragedy. In a manner it was not Mallare who became insane. It was his point of view that went mad. Although there are passages in the Journal that escape coherence, the greater part of the entries are simple almost to naiveté. They reveal an intellect able to adjust itself without complex uprootings to the phenomena engaging its energies. The first concrete evidence of the loathing for life that was to result in its own annihilation appears in a passage beginning abruptly—

"Most of all I like the trees when they are empty of leaves. Their wooden grimaces must aggravate the precisely featured houses of the town. People who see my work for the first

time grow indignant and call me sick and arti-
ficial. (Bilious critics!) But so are these trees.

"People think of art in terms of symmetry.
With a most amazing conceit they have decided
upon the contours of their bodies as the stand-
ards of beauty. Therefore I am pleased to look
at trees or at anything that grows, unhandi-
capped by the mediocritizing force of reason,
and note how contorted such things are."

Mallare's point of view toward his world—
the attitude that went mad—was nothing more
involved than his egoism. His infatuation with
self was destined to arrive at a peak on whose
height he became overcome with a dizziness.
He wrote in his Journal:

"It is unfortunate that I am a sculptor, a
mere artist. Art has become for me a tedious
decoration of my impotence. It is clear I should
have been a God. Then I could have had my
way with people. To shriek at them obliquely,
to curse at them through the medium of clay
figures, is a preposterous waste of time. A
wounded man groans. I, impaled by life, emit
statues.

"As a God, however, I would have found a diversion worthy my contempt. I would have made the bodies of people like their thoughts—crooked, twisted, bulbous. I would have given them faces resembling their emotions and converted the diseases of their souls into outline.

"What fatuous, little cylindrical creatures we humans are! With our exact and placid surfaces that we call beauty. And these grave and noble houses we erect!

"Yes, I ought to have been a God. I should have had my way with people then. I could have created a world whose horrors would have remained a consoling flattery to my cynicism."

There are entries that follow whose significance is lost in a serpentine rhetoric. They hint at nights of critical terrors. During the writing of them Mallare was engaged in a desperate pursuit of himself. He was escaping. He perceived his thoughts racing from his grasp like Maenads down a tangled slope. The dread of finding himself abandoned brought his will into life. If he were to go mad he would leap upon his mania and ride it—quietly into darkness. He would be a gay rider astride his own phantoms. Rather that than let the first insane capering of his intellect unhorse him and leave him gibbering after a vanished mount.

The incoherence of the Journal suddenly glides into an adagio. The panic has ended. And the lifeless eyed man again smiles triumphant out of the pages.

"My room is red. It is hung with red curtains. I have bought only red things to put in it. The sun coming through my red curtains reddens the air of the room.

"I prefer to live in this painted gloom because it is possible I hate the sunlight. I hate even my rivals the trees. Today I walked and found trees that resembled too closely people passing under them. One is impotent before such betrayal.

"But here in my rooms I find an almost complete annihilation of life. I am bored with inventing causes for my hatred. There is a diversion on earth called humanity—creatures full of enamelled lusts and arrogant decays who go about smiling and slyly obeying laws which protect them from each other. But they no longer divert me.

"They tell me of health and sanity. And I say sanity is the determined blindness which keeps us from seeing one another. More than that, of course: which keeps us from seeing ourselves. And health is the lame artifice of our bodies which keeps us from loathing one another. I see and I loathe. Yet I must beware of falling to sleep in explanations."

A month or a year may have passed between this and the continuation. Whatever the period, a clarity arrived. Mallare's mind grappling with the nightmare shadows engulfing it, distorted his reason to give them outline and was saved. The writing, however, becomes more labored in appearance as if the letters of words were now decorations in themselves.

"I have listened for years to the prattle of men who call themselves egoists. It is a

title by which they have sought to identify
me. To label a mystery suffices for its dis-
missal and thus they seek to dismiss me. There
is in egoism, however, a depth to which all
but myself are blind. I have found this depth
in myself and out of it rises a definition which
I must consider cautiously. There is but one
egoist and that is He who, intolerant of all
but Himself, sets out to destroy all but Himself. Egoism is the despairing effort of man
to return to his original Godhood; to return
to the undisputed and triumphant loneliness
which was His when as a Creator He moulded
the world to His whims and before He divided
Himself into the fragments of race and nature.
This is the explanation out of the depth.

"I must be cautious and keep my eyes
open. Secrets fly from the blind. Mount, I
say, and ride this secret and observe its direction. To return thus to Godhood means to
destroy All. And I were madder than I am
to play with this prospect, unless, perhaps,
there lie concealed in the elements, chemistries

still unknown which might be utilized for such destruction.

"As it is, I can with my thought deny and re-create and impose upon the world of reality a world of phantoms more pleasing to my nature. In my red room I sit and give birth to persuasive horrors. People shaped like dead trees. People freed from the monotonous hypocrisy with which a d e s p o n d e n t Nature endows their outlines. I have become aware that lobsters, beetles, crabs, and all the crustacean monsters that abound are not the abnormal accidents of creation, any more than were the animate gargoyles of prehistoric eras. They are the things which an Ego intent upon the diversion of truth fashioned in the beginning. Each thing to seem as each thing was. But the courage of this Ego deserted Him and He grew frightened when He came to give body to His most useless creation—Thought. And He compromised. Yes, I could live among people fashioned truthfully in their own images as are the crustaceans."

With this entry Mallare found it necessary to destroy the work his hands had created. He attacked the canvases and figures in his red room. Goliath who, preoccupied with his own deformities, had remained indifferent to his master, serving him faithfully however, listened to Mallare one night.

Sitting in the center of the room, his black hair grown into a long slant across his pale forehead, Mallare talked to his servant as a man, still asleep, reciting a dream.

"Here in this room, Goliath," he said, "are interesting works of art which I am about to destroy. On the canvases are dithyrambic burlesques in color, vicious fantasies, despairing caricatures. My fingers fashioned them and I remember the pleasant s l e e p e a c h brought me. But now I must beware of sleep. My egomania, like a swollen thing, has become impossible to articulate or to reduce to the impotent ironies of clay and paint. But I must beware of falling asleep under it.

"My friends have vanished as naturally as if by death. I have forbidden them to come.

This disturbs them, but see to it, Goliath, that no one ever enters my room unless I bring them. Frighten them if they come.

"Tonight, while there remained a little sanity, I had made up my mind to kill myself. But I have changed it. I will destroy instead my work. This is because I find the compromise easier and the destruction, perhaps, more interesting. I feel disinclined to abandon the things I loathe. The world with its nauseous swarm of life, its monstrous multiplications which are the eternal insult to the Omniscience I feel, still holds me. I am caught in a tangle and I remain suspended and inanimate, in the depth of a nightmare. But with your aid, Goliath, I will continue tenaciously mimicking an outward sanity so that people, when they see me, will go away happy in the assurance that I am as stupid as they."

Rising from his chair Mallare attacked, one by one, the canvases and statues. Goliath watched him in silence as he moved from pedestal to pedestal from which, like a company of inert monsters, arose figures in clay and bronze. The first of them was a man four feet in height but massive-seeming beyond its dimensions. Mallare had entitled it "The Lover."

Its legs were planted obliquely on the pedestal top, their ligaments wrenched into bizarre muscular patterns. Its body rose in an anatomical spiral. From its flattened pelvis that seemed like some evil bat stretched in flight, protruded a huge phallus. The head of the phallus was enlivened with the face of a saint. The eyes of this face were raised in pensive adoration. At the lower end of the phallus, the testicles were fashioned in the form of a short-necked pendulum arrested at the height of its swing. The hands of the figure clutched talon-like at the face and the head was thrown back as if broken at the neck. Its features were obliterated by the hands except for the mouth which was flung open in a skull-like laugh.

The figure on the whole was the flayed caricature of a man done so cunningly that

through the abortive hideousness of its outlines, its human character remained untouched.

Mallare swung the figure by its base
against the pedestal until it splintered and fell
to pieces. He stood whispering to himself—

"This was the lover. My statue of the
lover. Dead, now."

A dozen similar caricatures in clay and
bronze vanished under his attack. Standing
against the wall and blinking at the rutilant
glare of the room, Goliath the dwarf waited
nervously. He had become aware that his
master was acting strangely. A look of feroc-
ity slowly came into the deep black of his
face. His misshapen body trembled.

Mallare, the destruction ended, turned to
him.

"And finally a last figure," he murmured.
"Goliath, too. Do you agree, Goliath? You
will find a congenial company in the souls of
these friends I have butchered."

Goliath shook his head vigorously.

"Go 'way," he answered. Mallare nodded.

"Thanks," he smiled. "You reminded me in time. It is easy to mistake you for one of my creations. Although I never created such eyes, improbable eyes alive with murders. Go to bed."

Alone amid the wreckage, Mallare turned to his Journal. A precise smile was on his lips and his eyes slanted toward the debris on the floor as if he were watching the fragments, fearfully. His hair made a black triangle against his forehead. He began to write:

"I am too clever to go mad. To go mad is to succumb to the sanity of others. Since I avoid death, I must be wary of his misshapen brother. Yet, I can prove to my satisfaction tonight that I am mad. I have destroyed something. It was because the intricate presences of life awaken too many despairs in me.

"Now I am alone. I must be cautious of my thought. I feel words like rivals in my head. Alas, I must think in words. Words are the inevitable canonizations of life. But worse, they are property loaned me and not my own. I must have my own and live with it entirely. Yet there is some comfort in words. They are not entirely sullied by their promiscuity. Words are like nuts people pass each other without ever opening. The insides of words are often virginal. But many words— too many words—constitute intelligence and intelligence is the stupidity which enables man to imprison himself in lies.

"Years have passed and I still live. I do not look for death. Death is too simple a variant of destruction. My cleverness demands more of me than to destroy the world by hiding myself from it. And there is a song of windows in the high streets that sometimes relieves the black tension of my mind.

"It is important now that I retrace my way toward a makeshift of Omnipotence. But for this I will have to find a woman."

[II]

T was autumn. The air was colored like the face of a sick boy. Upon the streets rested a windless chill. The pavements were somber as during rain. There was an absence of illusion about buildings. They stood, high thrusts of brick, stone and glass, etched geometrically against a denuded sky.

Fantazius Mallare walked slowly toward his home. Over his head, trees without leaves stamped their gnarled and intricate contours on the shadowed air. A pallor covered the roofs. It was afternoon but a moon-like loneliness haunted the autumn windows.

Mallare lived in another world. Neither trees nor buildings conveyed themselves to his thought. Within his own world he was sane. His relation to the phantoms and ideas which peopled his mind was a lucid one. Mallare's world was his thought. He had retired within himself, dragging his senses after him.

The street through which he walked was like an unremembered dream. The faces that passed him vanished before his eyes. He walked, seeing nothing that was visible, hearing nothing that had sound. He had accomplished an annihilation.

Three months had passed since he had written in his Journal the command to find a woman. She was waiting for him now as he returned to his home. In the three months he had devoted himself to her transformation.

Mallare no longer raged. In the lucidity of his thought was a strange lapse. There had vanished from it all images of life except those of his own creation. His thought emptied of its projective sense, he found it difficult for him to translate his ideas in their relation to the world from which they had escaped. Yet he wrote in his Journal;

"I am aware of something that no longer lives in my mind. Dim outlines haunt me. Dead memories peer through the windows of my tower. Life grimaces vaguely on the edges of my madness. I can no longer see or understand. The world is a memory that expires under my thought. I am alone. Yet how much of me must still be the world! My dearest phantoms are, after all, no more than distorted reminiscences. I fear, alas, this is the truth. Yet it is pleasant to be alone with one's senses, to feel an independence."

The woman awaiting him was a curious creature. He had found her with a family of gypsies on the outskirts of the city. She was young—eighteen. His money had bought her release. She was called Rita and after two weeks she had agreed to come home with him. An old man in the caravan had said to her:

"This man is crazy. You can see that by his eyes and the way he walks. I have listened to him for two weeks and I know he is crazy. But you go with him, Rita. He is lonely and wants a woman. You go with him and obey him. You are young and he will teach you. Perhaps even you will fall in love with him. You are an ignorant child. Your mind is like a baby's. And perhaps you will not understand that he is crazy."

Among the gypsies with whom she had lived Rita was known as a simple one. She was never to be trusted to enter the cities they visited. She would remain with the wagons, helping to cook and wash. When men came to her in the evening and, sitting beside her, sang and played on guitars, she would listen for a moment and then run off. The old ones of the caravan said:

"She is not grown up. We must treat her like a child because there is still only a child's heart in her. She is beautiful but without sense. Some day she will make a good wife. But there is danger that she may give her body to strangers. Because she does not know about such things. We must be careful for her."

Sitting along the summer roads outside the city Mallare talked to the child. She listened without understanding but after days had passed, dreams of the man with the black hair slanting across his forehead came to her when she was alone. So when the Old One of the caravan said—

"You may go with this stranger. You can go away if you wish"; she nodded and smiled with happiness.

Mallare brought her home. And she had lived in the carnelian room that was colored like the inside of a Burgundy bottle ever since. Goliath was her slave. Mallare was her God.

At first he had said little to her. She wanted him to talk but he neither talked nor paid other attention. He brought her ribbons and dresses, trinkets, jewels, and playthings. She had a room in which to sleep but all day she sat in the room that was hung with heavy red curtains through which the sun filtered in a rouged and somber glow. Vermilion fabrics covered a long couch against the wall. Red carpets, red tapestries, tawny vases of brass inlaid with niello; crimsons and varying reds struck an insistent octave of color around her.

Mallare was absent during the days. She wondered where he went. He would return in the evenings with gifts. This had continued for a month. Then had begun a more curious existence.

One night Mallare had said to her:

"You must never talk to me any more but listen always to what I say. If you remain here you will have everything you wish. But you must not go outside. Do you understand?"

She closed her black eyes and nodded. He continued—

"I desire to make something out of you. If you stay here you will learn what I want you to be."

Thereafter he had sat for days at a time in the room with her. Goliath brought them food.

To Rita the smiling man who never ceased talking to her became like one of the Djinns the old ones of the caravan used to tell stories about, in the nights along the roads. The words he spoke became a languorous mist in her ears. She listened and understood only that this man with the black hair slanted across his forehead and the silent eyes, was talking to her. This made her happy.

At night she slept alone dreaming of the sound of his voice. Her heart became filled with awe. The strange room with its red colors was a Temple such as she had heard about but never seen. Mallare was a God who sat in its center and around whom grew a world of mysteries.

When she awoke her heart grew eager. Perhaps he would let her sit closer to him this new day. Perhaps his hands would touch her hair. She dreamed that some time he would play a guitar and sing to her as the men of the caravan used to do. But if that happened she would not run away as before. She would draw close to him and kiss his hands.

But the two months had passed without change. Except that the days became for Rita only the sound of a voice in her heart and the image of a face staring out of her secret thoughts.

She wore fine clothing. Rings crowded her fingers until her hands seemed little effigies of themselves. Her black hair was looped over her ears. A gold band was around it. She would have been happy if he had sat closer to her while he talked. Then the mystery of the words he spoke would not have separated them. Now she could lie on the couch, her head on her hand, her eyes burning and watch his lips move.

Her mind never asked what he was saying. His words carried him away. They were part of the mystery of him. Out of them she gleaned fugitive meanings as one recognizes for an instant familiar faces in a passing crowd. But she was content to lie watching him. A lethargy filled her. The days were like parts of a dream. At night, alone, she lay awake remembering them as a child playing with delicious fantasies.

She was asleep on the couch when Mallare came in. Goliath shuffled away as his master appeared. He had been standing in the center of the room, staring at the sleeping Rita, his eyes rolled up and his huge black head rigid.

She woke and Mallare smiled at her. Her eyes grew large and her red lips parted.

Mallare, seating himself, studied her with calm. She was his creation. He was giving her life. His mind was beginning to conceive her as a part of the phantoms that lived in him and that were his world. This illusion diverted him. His objective sense fast vanishing, he was gradually perceiving her as a tangible outline of his own hallucinations.

She was no longer the childish-minded gypsy girl he had found with the caravan. She was a fantasy of Mallare. There was no body to her but the body of his curious thoughts. A silent and adoring image of his brain stared

back at him from the vermilion couch. This
pleased him.

His madness had translated her into his
inner world. At moments a gleam of doubt disturbed his illusion. As he talked a conscious-
ness of her eyes would tangle his words. Her
eyes would become two dark intruders, and he
would rise and walk away.

"I must be careful," he would mutter
nervously.

Away from her the illusion would leave
him and his thought would consider lucidly
the situation it had created.

"My madness plays with a dangerous
toy," he pondered. "She is a woman and her
eyes are filled with desire. Perhaps she has not
even understood the things I have told her. I
must be careful, however, not to betray my
illusions with this lingering sanity. When I
am with her I conceive her a phantom—a
something which has stepped out of my madness to divert it. Her body becomes like one
of the dreams in my brain. Her little hands

reach like cobra heads among my intimacies. She is very beautiful that way. In my mind I caress her as a part of myself. I speak to her and it seems as if my words are talking to each other. Yet her eyes intrude and frighten me."

Now, as he studied her, the illusion he desired again filled him. His eyes turned inward saw only a dark-eyed phantom, a woman of mist that was no more than a hallucination drifting through his thought. He addressed this image of Rita softly.

"It is pleasant to be in love with you," he said. "Because love hitherto has been one of the abominations. In the world I have destroyed love existed. It was the foul paradox of egoism. Man, feeling suddenly the torment of his incompleteness, embraced woman. He was inspired by the mania to transform his desires into possessions.

"His heart taunted him. His brain filled with despairing vacuums. And he said to himself, 'I have become a deserted room. A woman will enter. Her beauty and desire will be gifts that will furnish me once more. She will be something I possess within myself.'

"In this illusion was contained the foul paradox of egoism. For in the world I have destroyed, egoism died in the embrace of love. The mania for possession which flattered man into seeking woman was no more than a shrewd mirage of his senses, that tricked him into the fornications necessary only incidentally to himself but vital to the world which he fancied love obliterated.

"For all these strenuous admirations of beauty—what are they but the subterfuges by which man hopefully conceals his lacking egoism from himself? He admires the tints of hair. His thought trembles before the curve of a neck. Graceful images unravel in his mind at the sight of a woman's breasts. To himself he declaims, 'I am in love with her. She is beautiful. I will take her beauty in my arms. There is an emptiness in me that clamors for the charm and mystery of this woman.'

"Accordingly he embraces her. There is tenderness between them. Their bodies, indeed, seem to have become overtones that mate in a delicious and inaudible melody. But this melody must be brought closer so that its beauty may be more definitely enjoyed. This melody must be played on instruments and not on thin air.

"And, selah! The egoist beautifying himself with love, finds himself removing his shoes, tearing off his underwear, fondling a warm thigh and steering his phallus toward its absurd destiny. The transvaluations—the ineffable and inarticulate mysteries he fancied himself embracing—turn out to be a woman with her legs wrapped around him. His desires for the infinite sate themselves in the feeble tickle of orgasm. Cerberus seduced from his Godhood by a dog biscuit!

"As for those animals whose egoism has never escaped their testicles, they are not to be spoken of as men. Their imagination discharges itself through their penis. They are the husbands in the world I have destroyed. They understand neither beauty nor disillusion. The vagina is a door at which they deliver regularly like industrious milkmen. They are the sexual workmen to whom fornication is as much a necessity as poverty is to incompetents.

"I alone have found the way in which to love. I love and grow richer. I am mad. Yet how admirable my madness is! My eyes and senses are enslaved by a radiant phantom. As I talk your outlines grow luminous. Your eyes become like conquered Satans. They crawl inside my brain like amorous spiders. Your lips are the libretto of a dream. Your breasts are little blind faces raised in prayer. Your body flutters like a rich curtain before the door of enchantments. I look within. Thus I possess you and my senses without leaving themselves, enter the infinity of my mind."

Mallare's eyes closed. He remained rigid in his chair. A murmur that Rita could no longer hear came from his lips, as if voices were speaking out of a depth.

"Rita . . . Rita," they said, "See, eyes prowling like golden tigers. Cobra hands playing over my soul. Mine . . . I walk with you through gardens, deeper and endless."

The murmur ended. Rita, watching from the couch, lay trembling. Warm tongues spoke within her body. Her breasts tightened until they felt impaled on their own nipples. Her child's mind was alive with impulses driving her like slow whips. She would crawl shivering to his feet. Her breasts would press their pain against his knees. Desire like an impossible anger filled her. She closed her eyes and felt herself moving from the couch. She would lie at his feet.

Her hands reached out. Mallare regarded her blankly for a moment. A wildness slowly filled his eyes. He sprang up. Goliath crouching in a corner of the dim room watched his master raise the velveted figure in his hands and fling it with a cry against the wall.

"Fool!" he shouted. "Intruder!"

Goliath cringed as his master rushed past him to the door. He listened to his feet flying down the stairs toward the night.

Rita lay with her head hanging over the couch. Her lips were opened. Her teeth gleamed like little deaths. She lay motionless as Mallare had flung her.

Goliath shuffled to the couch. His huge black face stared over her closed eyes.

{III}

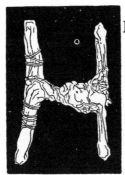E REMEMBERED that he had thrown the girl against the wall and he paused. The street was black. Great shadows balanced themselves on his eyes.

"I have escaped from myself," he muttered.

He stood trying to remember himself. But his mind was like a night. Shapes tip-toed through its dark. A hooded figure loomed in his mind. It swung toward him as if it were flying out of his eyes. Other figures swept by. They assumed strange postures as they passed. His thoughts regarded them tiredly. He desired to join the figures fleeing out of him. Then he would vanish with them.

"I am too clever for that," he murmured aloud. "Yet it would be pleasing. To think in dark, hooded figures; ah—they have adventures! And I would sit like a night alive with witches."

He stared with a smile at the street.

"I no longer see or understand," he whispered. His hands felt his sides.

"Yet here I am. There is a life within me that I dare not enter. I must remember this. Write 'Forbidden' over its black doors. To succumb to my madness would be to lose it."

He resumed his walk.

"She intruded," he remembered. "Perhaps I have killed her. That would be pleasant. Except that she was necessary as an image. I am the mirror and she is an image alive in me. Her desire is a happy shadow I embrace."

Mallare's eyes opened to the night.

"Strange," he thought, "I see and yet what I look at remains invisible. But tonight outlines dance. The night is a maniac suffering from ennui. His dark eyes are weary with the emptiness they create. Vainly he searches for life, his eyes devouring it, and leaving only his own image for him to contemplate.

"I am not so mad as that. Or I, too, would sit like the night gorged with monotonous shadows. Instead, I translate. A memory of sanity gives diverting outline to the shadows in me. I am not a maniac like the night. My mind closes like a darkness over the world but I enjoy myself walking amid insane houses, staring at windows that look like drunken octagons, observing lamp posts that simper with evil, promenading fan shaped streets that scribble themselves like arithmetic over my face.

"These must be the things I look at. But they are my improvement. The world is not so outrageous if one is sufficiently mad to pull it into taffy shapes and incredible scrawls.

"But I must be warned. My madness sought to avenge itself at her intrusion. It overcame me with its anger. She was not content to let me possess the beautiful image of her. Although I have explained the thing to her clearly. It is possible she does not understand. I will talk to her again with greater lucidity. I will tell her that I do not desire her except as a dream for my mirror. But I have said that to her."

Under the green-white sputter of a street lamp, Mallare halted. His mind was preoccupied with unraveling the mystery of Rita. He stood, a tall figure without a hat, a slant of black hair across his forehead, and ignoring eyes. A beggar in a ragged overcoat shuffled, head down, toward him.

"She is only a child," Mallare thought, "but it is evident that passion already lifts her breasts. Her simplicity is betrayed by incipient orgasms prowling for an outlet. This, she fancies, is love. It is fortunate she is a virgin. Still, I must not rely too greatly on that. For virginity is an insidious bed fellow for a maiden.

Forefingers and phallic shadows have ravished her in dreams. And if she is a virgin in spirit as well as body, she is still a woman—and therefore dangerous.

"Ah, what loathsome and lecherous mouths women are! Offering their urine ducts as a mystic Paradise! Stretching themselves on their backs and seducing egoists with the unctuous lie of possession. The mania for possession—that most refined of all instincts—the most heroic of insanities! How easily they circumvent it! To desire is merely to love. But to create in oneself the objects of desire—that is to be mad and above life. Beyond it.

"I must explain this to her. If she loves me well enough she will understand. All things are possible in love. I will explain to her that I possess her at will without the loathsome absurdities of sex."

The beggar paused and mumbled beside Mallare. Watery, reddened eyes waited patiently for the alms asked. Mallare had fallen into silence. He stood regarding the beggar intently. His thought labored for a moment, scratching in silence at doors swinging slowly shut. His thought withdrew and Mallare was alone.

He stood up tall and stern in a darkened chamber. His eyes stared intently at the figure of Rita. Her face, pale and alive, smiled imploring in the mendicant's place. He talked, but the beggar, still patient, heard no sound.

"You have followed me," said Mallare inside his chamber. "Very well. It is useless to explain matters to you. You pursue me with your lecherous body. I have warned you. Now I will kill you. I will take your throat in my hands and that will be an end of you. You will fall down."

The beggar uttered a cry of terror. Mallare's hands had reached suddenly to his throat and their fingers, like inviolable decisions, closed on it. The ragged one screamed. A man with a slant of black hair across his forehead who had stood smiling at him had without sound or warning reached out his hands to murder him. The beggar gasped and writhed, his eyes staring with horror into the immobile face of his assailant. And within himself Mallare continued the strange conversation.

"You see how simple it is," he said. "After you are dead I will continue to enjoy for a time the uninterrupted image of you. You will haunt my thought until you grow dim. But I will possess the vanishing shadow. . . . But now you die."

Mallare tightened his hold on the beggar's neck and the man's cries ended. His head fell forward. Mallare held the dead figure erect, shaking it gently and smiling at the one in his thought.

"Ah, Rita," he whispered, "it is over now."

His hands released the throat they were holding. The beggar fell to the ground. Mallare stared at the body and then knelt beside it. His hands passed over the dead face.

"Poor Rita," he continued. "No longer dangerous."

He bent over and kissed the matted hair of the dead man.

"Death," he said aloud as he rose, "is an easy friendship. You would have been sorry a moment ago. But now you are neither sorry nor glad. See, your body is a humble little gratitude."

Mallare walked away. His thought, like a cautious monitor, re-entered the doors that had closed upon it.

"Curious," he said aloud, "she followed me and I killed her. Madness is, alas, too logical. I remember almost nothing of the incident. It is a part of the shadows not of me. Still I know it exists. My hands feel tired. But there is nothing to regret. She came too close. And now she lies dead in a strange street. They will find her and perhaps ask me about it. What do I know? Nothing. My memory is innocent. It is after all my superior. I must remain, unquestioning, at its side. This is a pact."

He returned to his home. The familiar room greeted him like a friendship. He sat

down and closed his eyes. Goliath had gone to
bed. And she was no longer here.

His hands felt tired. He was alone again.
But he would remember her. Eyes like conquered Satans. They would crawl again like
spiders through his brain. Breasts like little
blind faces raised in prayer. Her body fluttering like a rich curtain before the door of
enchantments. These were still his.

"Tomorrow, Rita," he murmured aloud to
his thoughts.

A figure stirred on the couch. She had
watched him come in, his hair disheveled, his
body dragging. Her eyes had followed him as
he sat down. But she had waited motionless.
Perhaps he had come back to kill her. She lay
shivering. Then his voice called her name.

Standing slowly, Rita waited. He was
asleep but he had called her. She moved cautiously over the heavy carpet. Mallare opened
his eyes. He looked at the burning-eyed figure
of the girl his hands remembered having killed
in the strange street.

"A hallucination," his thought muttered. "But the dead do not come back."

The scene under the green-white street lamp played its swift detail through his mind again. He remembered the white throat, the pale, imploring face. A shudder passed his heart. He had murdered her. Yet here she stood once more, looking at him.

Mallare smiled.

"Ah," he thought. "Mad, completely mad. Yet it is not as unpleasant as I feared. Why, indeed, am I startled? This is what I desired. To create for myself out of myself. And here my phantoms have become so rich and strong that they confront me. I desired to be God. And I have answered my own prayer. It is an illusion. Its substance is only the life my madness gives it. Yet I, who am the companion of my madness, may enjoy it."

Rita shivered again as he laughed.

"Come closer," he whispered to her. "Or are you too timorous a hallucination, Rita?

Come closer and let me see. What a curious
sensation! To caress the figures of my madness!
Then there is no longer any sanity in me. For
my fingers are aware of hair. Ah, dear child,
Mallare is completely mad since at last his
senses betray him. But they betray him sweetly.
For though I babble to myself you have no
existence, though I smile at the thought of
caressing a phantom, my senses derive a mysterious pleasure from this contact with noth-
ingness. Curious . . . curious . . . come
closer, Rita. Now smile at me. Yes, your lips
move. You are an automaton born of my words.
Give me your hand. It is warm and trembling.
Ah, my phantom is in love with me. But that
love, too, is an illusion I create. No, do not
come too close. Let me grow accustomed first
to my madness. You are happy, eh? How marvelous your eyes! They were beautiful before
when they crawled like round spiders through
my brain. But elusive. They fled from me,
my madness pursuing them into dark, empty
corners.

"But now I have grown cleverer. It is necessary to be superbly clever in order to fool one's senses like this. But take off your clothes, little one. I want to see how clever I am. Has my phantom a body, too, or is it only a face and an illusion of fabric I have created? Your velvet dress, Rita, take it off. Ah, what a virginal phantom."

Rita, trembling before the gleam of the eyes that had opened to her, listened anxiously. An ecstasy drifted like a cloud over her senses. He had touched her. His hands had passed over her head as she had dreamed they might. His eyes were smiling with intimacy at her face. But he had warned her never to speak. She must not spoil it by speaking. She stood swaying before him.

"Your velvet dress," he repeated.

Her hands reached dreamily to her body. He would see now how beautiful she was. The men in the caravan had called her beautiful. But she had run from them. That was long ago. Now she would show him how the skin of her body looked, how her breasts made pretty curves, and how she had washed herself in the perfumes he had given her.

"Ah," murmured Mallare, his eyes filling with wonder. "How incredibly clever my madness has become! My little phantom undresses. Illusion—yet my conveniently stupid senses are deceived. But what delicious deception! See, her throat and breasts are white. Her body is white. I may reach out and touch the flesh of her thighs. I am as indecent as God for I have given her sex. But what a plagiarist I am! My phantom is as charming and naive as an art student's copy. Still, she is not a woman and therefore not hateful. Without life, even this may be considered entertaining."

His hands moved cautiously over her body, his fingers slipping experimentally over the flesh of her buttocks and thighs.

"Interesting," he smiled. "Like St. Anthony I create obalisques for my seduction. Ah, but there is a difference. This is mine . . . mine!"

His eyes gleamed with a quick frenzy at the naked figure.

"Speak. I desire you to speak, little one. If I can believe in the illusion of flesh and eager eyes, then I can believe in the illusion of sound. Come speak. I am at the mercy of my madness. If you speak to me, little one, I will understand. My stupid senses that retain their earthly logic will be ravished at the sound of your voice. But I will chuckle at my cleverness. Tell me, are you mine? Can you say, 'I am yours'? Can you give yourself to me and deceive me with the beautiful illusion of submission? Tell me. Speak to me."

Her eyes burning toward him, Rita nodded her head.

"Yours," she whispered. "Whatever you say, I am."

"Clever, clever," Mallare muttered, "it speaks to me and I hear. It says 'yours.' I become too involved. Or perhaps this is only a dream. Of course, what else can it be? Part of me has fallen asleep and is dreaming. And because I am mad I fancy myself awake. And my senses obey me. Desire whispers to them, 'Hear voices. See flesh. Feel desire,' and like five little awkward masochists they prostrate themselves before my madness.

"But my senses are of no great interest. There is this other—this mania of possession of which passion, compounded of all the senses, is but an unimportant fragment. I am a man with a woman inside him. I possess the secret of the hermaphroditic Gods. I am complete."

Rita kneeled beside him and his hands stroked her black hair. Her face remained raised in adoration. Mallare, observing her eyes, nodded satisfactions at them.

"Who but Mallare could have done this?" he whispered aloud to her. "Mallare, infatuated with himself, desires still a further adoration. So he creates infatuated phantoms. I am tired now. My hands are tired. Return, little one, to the couch of my madness and sleep for a time in its shadows."

Mallare shut his eyes and his hands dropped to his side. Rita arose and smiled at him. He had spoken strangely, but his words were no longer mysteries since he had caressed her. She would lie now at his feet as she had dreamed of doing. She stretched herself out on the thick carpet.

Her childish mind fondled its unexpected memories. He had looked at her body and spoken beautiful words to it. She remembered the talk of the old ones of the caravan. A woman belongs to a man. This meant that she belonged to him. She had said, "Yours."

Her face smiled itself to sleep.

[IV]

ROM the Journal of Mallare dated November.

"I no longer understand myself. My thoughts stretch themselves into baffling elasticities. My brain is a labyrinth through which reason searches in vain for itself. I walk cautiously. Yet I am lost.

"To think has become like adding a continually increasing column of figures. I sit and add. The figures will add up into a finite sum and this sum will be the understanding of myself. I apply myself carefully to each figure and say, 'two and three are five. Five and seven are twelve.' But as I reach what seems an end I find more figures waiting me.

"I can no longer add up the fragments or interpret them. I must be content now to sit and wait until this part of me—my relation to myself—splinters into fragments and I become a dice box shaking with mysterious and invisible combinations.

"It is the phantom Rita that is threatening to drive me into darkness. Since I murdered her in the street, the hallucination has become overwhelming. It is with me almost continually. When I open my eyes from sleep I find it waiting at my bed. The hallucination leaves me when I am outside, although at times a trace of it returns and I seem more to feel its presence within me than behold it with my senses.

"Yes, I am clinging desperately to these moments of objectivity which enable me to write. But even they threaten to betray me. For as I write doubts dance like macabre figures among my words. The very sentences seem to

stretch themselves into ridiculous postures.
And I must almost close my eyes and stumble
blindly through a storm of denouements.

"I desired to create for myself a world
within which I might love and hate—to be a
God lost within his dream. Madness was necessary, so I embraced it. But my dream becomes
the product of a Frankenstein. She—the hallucination—is more real to my senses than am
I. And I can no longer control her. My senses
are unfaithful to me. They philander clown-
ishly with this mirage of my thought. Then
what is there left? I. This grim figure stumbling with his head down through a storm of
denouements. I persist—an unwelcome visitor,
a bargain-hunting tourist in Bedlam. I remain.

"But it is a boast that laughs back at me.
For I will soon be a little plaything of my
phantom. Last night I walked until I thought
I had rid myself. Her eyes alone lingered. Her
hands moved like slow dancers. But I walked
and said to myself, 'I am tired of nonsense. I
am tired of this monotonous hallucination. At

least let me be unfaithful to my dream since I
am the God who created it.'

"I walked to the street where a month ago
she had followed me under the arc lamp. It
was cold and I grew tired. I came back to sleep.
'Gone, she is gone,' I whispered to myself. The
room appeared empty. I was cautious, knowing the ruses of this thing in my mind. For my
madness and I are no longer friends. My madness hides for me and plays tricks.

"But she returned. I smiled at her. It is
folly to grow angry with one's own hallucinations. That would be a double madness. As
she stood before me, my treacherous senses
leaped to their sterile feast. And I smiled.

" 'My egoism has betrayed me,' I reasoned. 'The love that gleams from the eyes of
this hallucination is the invention of my egoism. Alas, I love myself too much, for the
passion for Mallare with which my madness
endows this illusion of a woman, threatens me.
My senses have already abandoned me. They
no longer obey the direction of my will. And

I must stand like a scold, laughing and sneering at them as they yield themselves to her. She is more powerful, therefore, than I, even though her existence is no more than a shadow cast in front of my eyes.'

"I reasoned in this fashion and continued to smile. It would be best, perhaps, to humor her. Who knows but even hallucinations are subject to wiles and coquetry. A disturbing fancy, this—one of the distortions that insist upon raising their mocking heads from the midst of my cautious sentences.

"She came and knelt beside me and I shook my head at her. She was dressed in a gown I had never seen before. It was red. I spoke aloud and said—

"'See, how abominably clever I am. My madness is a jack of all trades. It makes new dresses for its phantoms. It arranges their coiffures. It even puts rouge on their cheeks.'"

"But as I talked her hands reached out to me. To look into her eyes that are always alive with flames is to succumb. For then I find myself dreaming my dream is not a dream. My senses clamor that I join them.

"'Forget. Forget,' they whisper, 'come with us.'

"But I chose to persist. I remain. To sit in an empty whorehouse and masturbate. . . . No! If this hallucination grows powerful enough to trick my senses into clownish fornications, let my madness enjoy them. Not I. We are no longer friends, my madness and I.

"She pressed her cheek against my leg. I could feel her body trembling.

"I remained motionless and spoke to her. 'Each night you grow bolder,' I said. 'I am no different from other Gods in that I seem to have endowed you with the instinct of profanation. But at least Eve did not turn on Jehovah with the whore tricks learned from His apple. There is consolation, however, in the fact that I, too, can remain indifferent. Indifference is the wisdom of God.

"'You may play with me. Yet I know that the burn of your hand on my body is an absurdity, of interest only to my idiot senses. My arms reach out to embrace you. Your breasts surprise my fingers. Come, sit in my lap if you wish. No, I would rather enjoy you as before—standing before me naked. Take off your clothes.'

"While I talked she clung to me. Her lips passed kisses over my face. I continued, however, to observe; to remain a spectator. She removed her clothes, tearing them from her body and laughing. And standing before me naked but for her black silk stockings and red slippers, she held out her arms. But I shook my head and smiled.

" 'I am the victim of an overwhelming desire to masturbate,' I said to her, 'since I find it difficult to resist you. But if I yield to the mysterious reality you have assumed I will become too grotesque for my vanity to tolerate. I will remain aware while possessing you that my penis is beating a ludicrous tattoo on a sofa cushion. I choose rather to emulate the pride of St. Anthony, who shrewdly refused to play the whoremonger with shadows.'

"I smiled at her and she laughed. She crouched on her feet staring up at me. Raising my eyes from her, I saw Goliath. He was standing in the curtains of his room, watching me with a curious, open-mouthed fury. I saw that the little monster was beginning to understand that I was mad, and this irritated me. There was danger in him, since even through his stupid head must have passed a wonder of what had happened to Rita.

"I frowned at Goliath and his head rolled frightenedly on his heavy shoulders.

"'Why do you bother me when I wish to be alone?' I cried. 'Go to your bed and leave me.'

"I stood up and went for him. His head fell and he dragged himself back into his room. This was, perhaps, the most curious thing in the incident. 'I am ashamed of being seen with this nude phantom,' I thought. For a moment the mad idea came to me that she was visible to Goliath—that he was watching us—me and this figment of mine. My anger was shame.

My senses are logical in their pretenses. How can I stand out against them, if they grow cleverer than I, more persuasive than I, and lead me finally into the total madness of accepting them as Mallare—the one Mallare, the lunatic who has escaped himself? I must not escape.

"When I returned she was still crouching on the floor. I decided to experiment. Perhaps there was still some lingering sense in me that would fail to succumb to this astonishing makebelieve.

"'Come here. On the couch,' I ordered her.

"She obeyed. She stretched herself out and I sat beside her. The odor of her body was distinct. Perfumes spread a clever gloss over the woman smell, the bitter salt odor that stirred from between her closed thighs. I smiled, for the logic of this illusion grows entertaining. But I had decided on experiments. My hands stroked her hair, feeling of its strands. My fingers pressed at the skull beneath the warm skin of her head. Then I held her breasts, that had once seemed to me like two little blind faces raised in prayer. But imagery no longer decorates my thought. My hallucination is no longer a weaver of magical phrases. But stark, real—its heart beating under ribs, its skin glowing with perspiration, its nipples standing out. As I caressed her I heard her say:

"'Yours. Yours. I am your woman.'

"Her thighs opened and her arms that had been held toward me fell to her sides. My hand slipped between. There was warm flesh. Yes, it was flesh to my mind. And I sat for moments allowing the illusion to stir a passion in me. I would throw myself on this thing, hold it in my arms, give myself to it. Where was the wrong in that, since it was only myself I ravished—a phantom mocking me behind my eyes?

"Goliath saved me. I saw him standing once more in the curtains of his room. His long arms were beating against his sides, the black fingers opening and shutting like frantic talons. He stood with his head rolling as if he were trying to stand erect. His eyes were insane.

"I sprang away, again pulled by the unmistakable emotion of shame. He glared at me for a moment, but as my hand caught his face he toppled over and lay whining. I picked him up and threw him into his bed and locked the door of his room.

"When I returned she still lay. Her eyes were closed. She looked at me and I saw she was weeping.

"'Since you are not to be reasoned out of existence, since you seem to resist what is left of my sanity—there is nothing to do but tolerate you.'

"I sat in my chair and spoke to her.

"'It will end in my loathing you,' I said. 'I created you in order to possess you beyond the realism of the senses. For a time your body was like a rich curtain before the door of enchantments which I might enter at will.

"'But there is no longer a door. Your body alone confronts me. In this way I am reduced to enjoying my dream with my senses. Then it means only that I have achieved nothing more by my madness than the privilege of masturbating with the aid of an erotic phantom.

"'Alas, the reason of it is clear. Man's fiber is fouled throughout with sex. I sought to emancipate myself from all relation to life. The delusion of my hopes is more to be pitied than the disorder of my vanity. For I see now that man is a collection of adjectives loaned to a phallus. His intellect is no more than a diverting hiatus between fornications. His soul, yes, his very egoism on which he prides himself, is a synthetic erection.

"'To possess! What a delusion! And for its sake I threw my genius away. I stripped the world from my eyes that it might not intrude upon the universe within me. A paradise in which I might strut alone. Possess myself. Yes, and here I am, aware at last of folly. For my senses belong to life. And though I buried myself in a madness deeper than night, they would still cling to me. Though I castrated myself, they would remain—five invisible testicles. It is impossible to possess. Folly to attempt. As long as the senses remain life clings like a dead whore to my darkness. Even my madness that I prided myself upon is a babbling witch astride a phallus, her lips bending over it with grewsome hungers.

" 'There is only one castration—death. What am I now? Mad? Yes. And worse. Disillusioned. I have closeted myself with a lecherous animal and it turns on me. That is the reward of the privacy I hungered after.

" 'And you who lie and weep on a couch are no longer the dream of a God, but the crude marionette created by lust for its own diversion. I thought only to go mad. But I see I have become an idiot.'

"There was no more to say. Her weeping ended and she vanished. But she will return. In my sleep her outline wanders like an amorous ghost haunting the grave of my senses. Ah, I must be cautious now, more cautious, always cautious. It would be too easy to yield. And if

I yielded and returned again my defeat would be unbearable. I think it is easier to die. Death is no more than a premature torment. Its name alone is a suffering. Its reality but a final illusion.

"But I persist. I still remain. There is a rhythm to things that still seduces me. A gentle curiosity that gives the lie to my bewilderment. I sit, an audience, shedding crocodile tears at a melodrama.

"Tomorrow . . . tomorrow. Who can think that word is still himself? What difference does it make if I grow uncomfortable and swollen with illusions? I persist. And who knows but tomorrow will be a door in my labyrinth . . . a bottom to this pit into which I have fallen?"

[V]

ROM the Journal of Mallare dated December.

"Her murder was simple. We stood under an arc lamp and my hands killed her. I remember her face looking imploringly at me. And when I went away I leaned over and kissed her hair. She was dead in the street. It was simple.

"Now I must kill again. It is no longer simple. I must teach her to hate me. She will vanish then. It is clear in my thought. My hands are useless against her now. I have held them about her neck and she laughs.

"All day she runs around in the room. At night she comes to my bed. Her hands wake me up. She plays with me. I lie thinking how she may be murdered this second time. She has grown loathsome. I allow her to cover my body with kisses and listen to her laughter. Pollutions result. I am powerless against her lips and terrible fingers. She devours me night after night like a succubus. I lie and masturbate with a phantom.

"But I will discover a way to kill this thing. I close my eyes and lie powerless while she repeats the refrain I once taught her. 'Yours . . . yours. I am your woman.'

"I have hurled her out of bed, hurled her body against the wall. She continues to laugh like a child. I think of her as real. Goliath knows I am mad. He watches me while I struggle with this thing. He is filled with terror. I have told him to go, but he remains.

"She sleeps in the bed that Rita used. I have seen her there. Stood beside her listening to her breathe. If I die she will pursue me in

death. She is more real than I. I must kill her.
My hands have never touched her since the
night on the couch. I have kept myself intact.
I still remain. She is a virgin. My thought is
mad. It plays with the idea of fornication.
Once, screams frightened her out of my bed. I
lay unable to resist. My body reached toward
her. An anger that was like death blinded me.
I cried out and saved myself. My thought crept
back from the madness. I called myself back.

"I can no longer close my eyes to her. She
grimaces in the dark. And she is at my heels in
the street. I have decided there is a way to rid
myself of her.

"Mallare . . . Mallare is no more. Madness jostles him off the scene. He annihilated
a world and a new monster sprang up in its
place.

"My words return. Ah, tired warriors
covered with the grime of battle—they troop
back to my mind out of the dark. Mallare
returns. But what a caricature! See him like
a fanatic priest driving the devil out of his
soul with whips.

"This would be a God, this hermaphroditic prostitute who fondles himself at night. Mallare . . . weep. Whips will not rid you of this monster. Mallare, the plaything.

"But there is a way to be rid of her. Hate will darken the gleam of her body. She will vanish. But do I hate her? My madness is infatuated since it makes her so radiant. And who am I that I laugh at my madness? It is I who am insane. Not this other Eden maker whose mania I applauded. I, Mallare, tear at my hair.

"I look in the mirror over my bed. Eyes red and gleaming look back at me. This is my face, but I am no longer there. And whose are these eyes looking back at me? The eyes of Mallare's friend, red and gleaming. His friend who betrayed him. Hair slanting over a forehead. Mouth wide and thin. No longer mine. They belong to the mirror. Mallare's words whimper before them.

"Weep . . . weep, impotent one. The feet of your madness walk solemnly over you.

They kick gravely at a carcass. Lie beneath them and watch Mallare dance away, whirl away with lecherous shadows in his arms. But she will die too. I am thinking of death. Mallare the egoist asks alms of death!

"Windows break inside me. I look out of broken windows. I am gone and away. Empty rooms. My hands feel walls. Mallare asks pity of darkness. Pity him."

[VI]

HE sat looking out of the window. He had gone away early in the morning. It was growing dark now. The cold street dwindled. Windows lighted up. People that looked from the distance like black toys moved through the darkening street.

She could tell when he came because his walk was different. The hours built pointed roofs to her dream. She played behind happy walls but her eyes remained outside, watching from the window.

This was part of a game—to hide away and wait. To put on her clothes carefully in the morning; bright silks and petticoats and a dress on top; jewels on her fingers; bracelets and earrings; gold bands through her hair. To make her cheeks red and paint black lines in her eyes; then paint her lips and fingers red—these things hid her. She must be hidden when he came—concealed behind paints and clothes so that when he looked at her it would be someone else he saw.

A tall man with black hair. His face was white. His eyes were silent and hidden. But when they looked at her they screeched like parrots. They ruffled up and yellow points came into them.

He liked to walk up and down pretending she was nowhere, pretending there was no Rita, pretending he was looking for her. Then she ran around and one by one she took off the things—the dress, the petticoats, the silks, the jewels and bracelets and gold bands. Each one she took off was for him. It was a game. She came out of hiding places. Each one she took off was a secret she confessed to him.

She sat at the window dreaming of the ways she belonged to him. Her thought was a pantomime which prostrated itself before his memory. She remembered sacrifices. . . . He would lie cold in his bed. Then she crawled to his side. She dared not look at his eyes. They were above her and kept themselves hidden. She vanished before the thought of them.

Then his body grew warm under her hands. Her lips made his body tremble. He was white and naked like her. He was a fire to which she fed herself. The moment came when there was no longer any Rita. A little ember lay burning happily in his passion.

When he fell asleep she went away. In her own bed she lay dreaming words that were like hiding places. Only he could lure her out of them. After he fell asleep she carried memories of him into herself. . . . He had smiled. His body had shivered. His fingers had clutched at her face. He had picked her up and fought with her. When he did this it was as if he lifted her to his eyes and she could look at him—as if the wind lifted the flames about.

The street was dark. But he would come soon. He only stayed away till it grew dark. Now it was his time again. The street and all the lights would open the door and come into the room. And she would be waiting, hidden away. It was exciting to wait. It was the way he kissed her—by making her wait and pretending when he came that there was no Rita.

The night was like a story that frightened. As she watched from the window she remembered the caravan along the roads. Fires and dark faces and red handkerchiefs. The night along the roads changed the trees into birds that flew away. The wagons went to sleep. Everyone slept but Rita. The horses had dreams and whispered to themselves.

Along the roads where the caravan stopped there would be a fire at night to watch. Rita sat alone looking at the flames. Dreams came out of the fire and walked away. Then, hours afterward, they came back when the fire was low. They stood around the coals and finally crawled into the ground. Darkness remained.

The wagons became ghosts. She grew sad and wanted to go away with the night like the dreams that crept back into the dead fire.

Now his eyes were like the hiding places she had wished. She trembled. He was coming. She could see him out of the window, walking slowly in the street below. She closed her eyes.

The door opened and her heart bowed itself. Her fingers, stiffened with colored rings, pressed at her breasts. Now there was a game to play. He walked up and down pretending Rita was hidden. He was cold and far away. His face walked like a dead man back and forth in the room. Goliath shuffled as fast as he could and hid himself in the curtains. She crouched in the chair, her knees drawn up, her eyes cringing with delight.

She could watch his face. When he was far away she had further to go to reach him, and each step was like a kiss she gave him. His anger, his words, his cold face and his hands

striking her were wild roads down which she
ran toward a fire that waited.

He paid no attention but walked up and
down and his eyes ignored her. But he would
begin to talk soon. She would undress for him.
One by one, rings, bands of gold, silks and petticoats—each that came off was like a part of her
already burning.

She stood up naked. Only she was left
now. Her body caressed her with its desires.
She must go on undressing. There was something more to give him. She would remove
something of herself—her arms, her breasts,
her white thighs. She gave these to him with
her dresses and jewels. They were things for
him to burn up.

He was looking at her because she had
crawled to his feet. This was when he began to
talk to her—when she placed her arms around
his feet and bent her head to the floor.

"Yours," she whispered.

He was motionless and far away and tall
above her. He stood like the night. His white

face was the cold moon. She waited and heard the wind blow against the windows. She waited for him to grow warm.

His hands lifted her up. He held them around her neck, his fingers tightening. She opened her eyes and loved him. He talked to her. She listened and wished to die in his hands, if he desired her, if it would make his eyes smile at her.

But his fingers loosened and he threw her down. She lay smiling on the floor as he walked away. He went on talking, louder and louder. His voice was like a sword swinging. He was angry. His words were soft and quick.

She looked up only when he laughed. He was standing against the red curtains laughing. His finger was pointing to her. He stood watching her with his eyes screeching like parrots and laughing as he pointed.

Kneeling, she covered her face with her hands. His laughter came nearer. His hands began to strike. Pain leaped to greet them. Pain, like wings, raised her body to his eyes.

His hands were striking and tearing. They played a game with her body.

Candles lighted in her head. He was laughing and throwing himself against her. She felt blood come out of her and cover her with little flames. But he would let her come close soon. After he had struck her and become like a fire she would crawl close to him and he would let her give herself, what was left of herself.

His hands knocked her down again and she lay without moving. He was still laughing and pulling at her. She kneeled and covered her face. Her head kept nodding at him.

Now she would die. He would devour her. Her body fell and rose as if he were swinging her around his head. His hands drove nails through her breasts. Her voice ran away from her and screamed. But she continued to nod her head and to come toward him out of the hiding places. His blows were binding her body with red ropes. But soon she would lie against him and give herself to his passion.

She would feel his body burning from the blows he had given her. She closed her eyes and screamed. He grew larger and she was no longer able to understand the pain. . . .

When she awoke Goliath was bending over her. He was whispering excitedly. Sunlight made red shadows in the room.

"Where is he?" she asked.

She slid to the floor and then stood up carefully. Pain halted her and she moaned. But her eyes continued to hunt the room.

"Where is he?" she asked again.

Goliath watched her and his head rolled excitedly. She straightened and dragged herself to the door of his room. It was empty.

"Mallare," she cried. Her hands beat against her head, "Mallare."

Goliath remained watching her naked figure stumbling through the rooms as she called the name. She returned to the couch and threw herself face down. She lay moaning and tearing the cushions with her fingers.

He had gone away. He had beaten her not because he loved. He hated her. And he had taken himself away from her. She understood. He no longer wanted her. He had laughed and tried to kill her.

With a scream she rushed into his bedroom and threw herself against the unused pillows. Her arms struck at them. She began to talk aloud in the language she knew.

"Gone away, gone away," she cried. "I am yours and you gone away."

But words were too involved. She beat at the pillows and screamed. When he came back she would kill him. While he sat in his chair writing she would creep close and drive a knife. That was what would happen to him because he no longer loved her and because he had beaten her to say goodbye.

It was day outside. When it grew dark again he would come back. She would wait, but not as before. She was no longer his.

In her room Rita bathed herself and searched for her old clothes. She found them hidden—the wide dress with red and yellow stripes, the many blue and scarlet petticoats that she had worn when he brought her home from the caravan; the long black earrings, the green and orange shawl for her head. She put these on. They hid the vivid marks on her body.

Dressed in her gypsy clothes she came into the room again. It would be long to wait. But darkness would come and then he would open the door again. She lay down on the couch and sighed.

[VII]

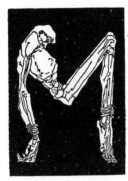ALLARE, wrapped in a
heavy overcoat, his hands in
thick gloves, walked from
his door into the street. The
cold straightened him. The
deserted night mirrored
itself in a thin coating of
snow that overlay the roof-
tops.

"They sleep," he thought. His head bent
toward the wind. "The streets are empty. The
night is mine. I must think of what has happened. There is something inexplicable in
what has happened. My hands fought with a
phantom. That, of course, is nonsense.

"How do I know my hands fought?
Merely because I remember them striking.

Yet that may have been an illusion too! Then why are my hands tired? Why do my arms ache? Another illusion, of course. Logic is independent of truth. Logic is the persuasive repetition of ideas by which man hypnotizes himself. I must beware of logic. It will but tie me hopelessly to hallucination. I must think without evidence. I do not know anything. What I see, hear, smell, touch is nothing. I can no longer summon my senses as witnesses.

"And is that unusual? I must sink to moralizings in order to understand myself. What is reality but the habit of illusion. Man sees the unexpected once and identifies it as hallucination. He sees it twice and calls it phenomenon. But if he acquired the habit of seeing the unexpected, he accepts it as reality.

"In the same manner in which he builds phantoms into furniture, converts his Gods into sciences, his myths into laws; in that way he also reduces his furniture into phantoms. He converts his emotions into music, his nervous disorders into literature, his three elemental

desires into thought. He is continually holding a mirror to nature and worshipping the
childish phantoms within the mirror.

"This is the basis of egoism—the mania
to change realities into unreality. Because
man is the tool of reality. Of unreality he is
the God. It is this desire to dominate which
inspires him to avoid truths over which he has
no sway and to invent myths. Gods and virtues
over which he may set himself up as creator
and policeman. It is this which causes him to
cloud the simplicities of nature in a maze of
interpretations. It is by his interpretations that
he achieves the illusion of importance. Ignored
by the planets, he invents the myth of mathe-
matics and reduces the universe to a succession
of fractions and Greek letters on a blackboard.

"This, of course, for man the egoist. The
more humorous spectacle is the one in which
man finds himself awed by his own lies. His
Gods, his myths, his phantoms come home to
roost. He stands blinking in a veritable storm
of lies. His yesterday's lies, his today's lies, his
tomorrow's lies—all his obsolete interpreta-

tions, his canonized interpretations; all his systems, his philosophies; all his Gods and Phantoms—these riot and war around him. Error endlessly assassinates itself in a futile effort to escape its immortality.

"And in the midst of this horrendous confusion, stands man—naive and powerless. But he has his sanity. He blows it up carefully like a soap bubble and strikes a defiant posture in its center. And against the walls of his bubble, his phantoms storm in vain. Within his bubble he proceeds calmly to assert himself."

It was snowing. The night, white with snow, stared like a blind man. A phantom world hung in the air. Houses and street withdrew silently. The snow covered them. Mallare walked on, staring into the heavy weave of flakes.

"A great white leopard prowling silently," he murmured. "It snows. The moon has come down and walks beside me. The wind blows and the moon gallops away on a white horse. A gentle annihilation. The night has fallen asleep and this is a dream that pirouettes in its head. The street becomes a bridal couch.

"Ah, the snow is like my madness. It snows, snows. I climb silently among soft branches and white leaves. Delirium sleeps with a finger to its pale lips. I must continue to think. The storm hangs like a forgotten sorrow in my heart. But my thought persists. It crawls like a little wind through the forgotten storm. It rides carefully from flake to flake.

"I overtake myself. What a quaint imbecile I am. Or rather, was. In my effort to emancipate myself from life, I succeeded only in handing myself over to my senses. And my senses, I perceive, belong not to me but to the procreative principles of biology. They have been loaned to me by a master chemist. When I die my cherished soul will disintegrate into nothing. It will become a useless thing. It will unquestionably go to a Heaven which is as non-existent as itself. Heaven is the emptiness into which souls vanish. Very good. But my senses, these are immortal. They will, in some inexplicable way, I am certain, continue their idiot career.

"I must consider them. I have learned one thing. They are indifferent to reality and unreality. They contain life within themselves. All that exists outside them is extraneous— shadows among which they divert themselves.

"The hallucination that overpowered me but never seduced my intelligence became a reality to them. She was a shadow with which my senses diverted themselves. Then why do I look upon the business as illogical? The illogical thing is not that I feel tired from striking her who had no tangible existence, but that I should be able to reason beyond the reach of my senses. Yes, that I should succeed in wresting them from their prey. For the shadows with which the senses divert themselves are tyrants they may never hope to abandon. Man is at the mercy of his phantoms. Behold, I arrive at a conclusion which means I am bored with the subject.

"I prefer the snow. But there is time for the snow. I must establish premises. Climb out of the abyss on a ladder of premises. What did I say about logic? Oh, yes, the persuasive repetition. One flake remains invisible. A thousand flakes are of no account. It is only when the flakes repeat themselves too endlessly for my eye to distinguish that I finally ignore them and walk contentedly in a storm. Thus with logic. When I have surrounded myself with an infinity of assurances, my error vanishes in the constant repetition of itself. And I am reassured. And sane.

"Yet I must think simply. The snow seduces me into fellow labyrinths. I've destroyed her. My senses were in love with her. They responded to her kisses. She was a Thought able to ravish my body. This is what the pathologists would identify as a triumph of the psychic sex center. What charming palaverers—the pathologists! Man crawls in a circle around himself and fancies himself an invader—a pathologist.

"A matter of no interest. What I have done, as the Christian Scientists ably put it, is to rid myself of this Thought. But why was it necessary to strike at it with my hands, to tear it with my fingers? This worries me. But did I do these things? I must convince myself that I didn't. I remember sinking my hands into her body, pulling at her flesh. I remember blows given. She screamed. I struck her and flung her down. These things I recall.

"But they do not interfere with my convictions. For of what are they proof? The blows I gave were no more than a shrewd make-believe. To my senses she was real, and it was necessary therefore to destroy her realistically. It was easy for my mind to ignore this Thought. I was never its victim. I merely created it. My senses that belong to life and not to me, however, became victimized.

"I do not recall myself as a spectator of the struggle. I remember it now as I might remember participating in an honest fight. A very clever ruse. It is evident I loaned myself. I surrendered adroitly to my idiotic senses. Therefore for that hour I was completely mad.

What happened in the room? Ah, what a grotesque memory it makes. Mallare knocking his fists against the air. Mallare throwing himself around like an epileptic. Sinking his fingers into nothing—a shadow boxer pummelling frenziedly at space. That was madness.

"But it served its purpose. For I've destroyed her. Rita, Rita is gone. Yet there's a curious twist in that. I am lacking one memory. One very important memory hides from me. I calculate its time and place, but, like a recalcitrant comet, it fails to enter the appointed void. Alas, I no longer remember killing her in the street.

"But I am certain I did. Why, certain? Because my logic establishes the fact. Still, I would feel better about something, if my memory were more docile. But what is memory? The soul of dead illusion. Since it withholds itself, I will create a memory.

"There was a lamp shining over my head. I was walking. And then I stood still. Oh, yes, shadows. I grew eloquent with shadows. And

she appeared in the midst of this eloquence.
My hands choked her. She had followed me
into the street and I choked her. But I do not
remember this. At least, the thing grows elusive and unsatisfactory. Why? Ah, the snow
covers me. I will cover my confusion with a
sigh like the snow.

"No, I see the thing now. Was she ever
real? There were gypsy wagons and an old
man. A camp fire and this girl with the green
and orange shawl. Yes, these were realities.
But how do I know? Hm, I place my finger
on the sore spot. There is a point where reality
and unreality meet. And this point has vanished from my mind. I pursue it. A matter of
remarkable importance. It evades me; therefore I will arbitrarily locate it. The point
between reality and unreality is the arc lamp
in the street. Up to that point Rita was real. I
killed her at that point and she became unreal.
This statement cures me. Nevertheless, my
sanity is a myth. I have invented it, by arbitrarily identifying the moment of its departure.
But it is better that way than to blunder on

without knowing how mad I am or whether I am mad at all, or whether I ever have been mad. A lie believed in is an antidote for confusion.

"It doesn't matter. Excellent logic. She is destroyed. And I am none the worse, except for a disillusion more—and an uncertainty. My uncertainty is removed by logic, or at least concealed by it. And I am sane. I return to life—another Napoleon walking backwards. My experiments have led me around a circle. I meet myself where I started, but naked of hopes.

"It snows and I am amiable. Something has happened. My hatred, where is that? This street is pleasant. The light of the snow cheers me. I am, in fact, buoyant. Ah, I understand. A balloon come down to earth and vain once more of its buoyancy—its ability to bob along the pavement.

"It is curious. I delude myself that I am thinking. But my alleged thoughts do not further my ideas. They merely convert them into little pictures easy for me to understand and diverting to look at.

"Still, if I am happy . . . but how does one know one is happy? I suspect my happiness. It is a clown's suit in which my mourning disguises itself. Mallare has fallen out of his black heaven. And he picks himself up like a good burgher. He grunts and chuckles and looks at the skies, alas, without curiosity. Lucifer, fallen, finds diversion as a janitor in red tights. Ergo, I have proved something. I am in Hell and with Lucifer I know its secret—happiness.

"Where is Mallare who fancied himself a madman? Who sought to climb over his senses and found himself impaled by a tower of Babel? Where are his angers, his disgusts that were the noble shadows thrown by his egoism to blot out a world? Ballad of rhetorical questions. My vanity preens itself with reminiscenses. I smile. I am depressed and content. Answers whisper. Mallare is on his feet. His experiments are ended. His mania to possess himself is a snow that falls forgotten in his past. Vale, the lunatic. Vale, the man in the moon. Ave, Mallare.

"It snows. I walk. I think. I smile. And this too for a time is a diversion—that people no longer distract me. I carelessly restore the world. Let there be people, I say. And, alas, there are. I abdicate. I hand my Godhood back to the race.

"Morning begins like another snow in the distance. Ah, here comes one tired-eyed out of a house. It is astounding to think that he is human like myself. He and I are actors in the same play, yet ignorant of each other's lines. But I may guess at his part. He is frightened. He looks furtively toward me. And he walks rather lamely. Aha, a fornicator! He has left a warm bed, illegally occupied for the night. A woman in a rumpled night dress moaned under him. The plot is simple. How pleasing it was for a moment. She came so close. She was like an incredibly intimate secret. He gasped physiological instructions. And—finis! The captains and the kings depart. The recessional of the douche! Do you love me yet, do you love me yet?

"And now he walks in the cold street. He must hurry away. There are complications, but they make a minor drama. Off stage business. He is aware of contrasts. A moment ago—her arms, her gasps. A moment ago warmth, intimacy. And now, the snow, the cold, and life. Memory like fool's gold jingles in his pocket. Life is real, life is earnest. He regrets his orgasms. They will interfere with business.

"The male rampant! What a sinister comedian! The mythical despoiler. Hm, his head bows down. The snow disturbs him. Sad, weary, remorseful, he drags himself home. He has lessened his virility and it worries him. There is a plot in this. Some day I will write it out—a love story of the sexes. Poor, weary one, he has enriched Delilah.

"Ah, I am amused. It will be pleasant to observe people once more. Sanity has its rewards. Its laughter is a charming hint of madness that one may enjoy harmlessly.

"What a lecherous spectacle a row of dark houses is! Bedrooms filled with bodies— incredible nudities. Bed springs creaking. The hour of asterisks. Window blinds down. Doors locked. Lights out. The city lingers in the snow like a feeble burlesque. Houses and shops and street car tracks gesture reprovingly. Civilization bows its head in the night like an abandoned bride. Man, like an ape hunting fleas, preoccupies himself again with his nerve centers.

"Darkened houses, silence—Rabelais and Boccacio debate the immaculate conception. Eros, patron saint of the laundryman, conducts ancient rituals.

"Ah, these indefatigable and unctuous fornicators, rolling their eyes piously between orgasms; embroidering noble mottoes on their pleasure towels! [These prim exquisites, carefully and with raised eyebrows, folding their toilet paper into proper squares!] Who can be

angry with them? God drove them out of
Paradise—punishment enough. They revenge
themselves with a monotonous enthusiasm. Ah,
these fellatian moralists! It is folly to take
their hypocricies to heart. The plot is too delicious for tears. These two-fisted citizens, these
purity braggarts masturbating with one finger
unemployed and pointing scornfully at their
neighbors!

"Charming street. It offers consolations,
simple ones, to be sure. But nevertheless, consolations. My madness was not as mad as this
dark street. This is a prettier witches' night
than the one I aspired to. I am amused and
my amusement is an insult that inspires me. If
one cannot become God, one can at least sit and
sneer happily at the handiwork of his rival.

"The dawn comes into my head. Poor
Mallare, who must readjust his vocabulary to
coherences. The night flies away. How simple
this little scene becomes. Mysteries vanish.
Doors open. Window blinds raise themselves.
And now people stick their heads out into the

cold. Wagons, trucks, crowds begin. They hurry to work, older by a night.

"My sanity laughs at them, but sadly. I detect an obligato to my mirth. The comedy is poignant only because I am a part of it. These hurrying ones with their tired faces and eager shoulders are my brothers and sisters sharing with me the spectacle they make. They are a disillusioning mirror in which I see myself a million times. Yes, they look back at me, and their weariness, their hopelessness saddens me. Man sees himself by gazing into the world—and is overcome. It is only a lunatic who can keep merry in the face of so monstrous an image.

"My happiness is without merriment. I return quickly. I have already the habit of coherence. In a few hours I will go back again and begin with canvas and paint once more. My madness is a lost argument. I am a little tired. But, alas, he who has danced and slept with Medusa goes home weary.

"It will take time before my amusement ripens into rages. And without rages work is impossible. I will wait. Now I am too indifferent for anything but happiness. It is easy to walk and forget one's self and one's senses. It will come back. Mallare will return and expend himself naively in decorations once more.

"When I am strong again I will hunt up a woman. Poor Rita, whom I have murdered twice, illustrating the paradox of possession. Man, the slave of his senses, possesses only what his five masters offer him as gifts.

"I will find a clever one this time whom jests do not frighten. One who does not burn incense before her vagina and cover it with an altar piece. How unctuously women embrace ideas which increase the value and importance of their urinal ducts! Modesty, morality, prurience, piety, are the effulgent underwear behind which they increase the mystery and charm of the mons veneris. Alas, they are the artists of sex and not men. Man has even thrown away the seductive cod-piece. The origins of ideas are varied and multiple. But whatever their origins, it is women who utilize them. What an incredible sex! Vaginomaniacs.

"I will hunt up a vulgar woman, one who does not piously regard her vulva as an orifice to be approached with Gregorian chants. I must be careful to avoid those veteran masturbators marching heroically under the gonfalons of virginity. It is a difficult business, finding a woman. A modest one will offend my intellect. A shameless one will harass my virility. A stupid one will be unable to appreciate my largess. An intelligent one will penetrate my impotency.

"But why women? The devil take them all. I am almost tired of the disillusions they have to offer. The homely ones go away grateful for something they never received. The pretty ones go away chuckling secretly over something they never gave. It is a confused and unintelligible waste of time. It will be enough to paint, to talk, to sip tea, to wander about proselyting in behalf of improvised Gods. I will divert myself, making love to women out of range of their bedrooms. I will engage them conversationally and ravish them with erect and quivering adjectives. It is not necessary to undress a woman to know her. She reveals herself almost as piquantly in moods. I will be the father of moods. And, as a recreation, I will sit and watch the days in their unchanging flight. I bristle with rhetoric. It is a symptom of sanity. I am grateful for this ability to bore myself."

It was morning. Mallare paused against a window. He stood, staring into the life of the street. His eyes were drawn and the corners of his wide, thin mouth smiled feebly.

Snow was falling. The morning dissolved itself. Traffic drifted busily and without sound behind the snow—an excited pantomime that filled the air with misplaced, ventriloquial whispers.

Mallare remained smiling into the gentle storm. Snow covered his head and shoulder.

"The snow falls," he thought tiredly. "It snows, snows. White flakes lose themselves and are grateful for the earth. An invisible ending that flatters them. Well, I have walked all night and rid myself of wisdoms. I am hungry. It's possible I haven't eaten for months. In order to eat, however, I need money."

He slipped one of the gloves from his hand and felt in his pocket. A satisfied smile came to his eyes.

"Excellent," he thought. "Or I would have celebrated my sanity by starving to death."

Withdrawing his hand from his pocket, he found himself regarding it. It grinned back at him like a stranger. It was red.

"Blood," he murmured. His eyes glanced quickly around and he replaced the glove. He continued to walk.

"Blood," he repeated to himself. The word made an ending in his thought. He walked slowly staring at it. His silence lifted. A voice crept into him and began to speak from a distance.

"Careful," it murmured. "Be cautious. Remember you were mad. You had almost forgotten. There is something to think about, now. You will walk slowly and think. It's not as easy as it seemed. Be careful.

"Your fists fought with a phantom. Blows, wild blows. The grotesque memory—the madman pummelling the air. That was you. And your hands are bruised. They've been bleeding. Her breasts and head were something else. Your fists struck mercilessly at chairs and walls. When your hands are washed you will find bruises over them that have been bleeding."

He walked on nodding his head slowly. Later he stopped. The snow was piling itself over the grass of a small park. The swollen shapes of trees and benches rested in the storm.

Mallare sat down on a bench and removed his gloves. Both hands were red. Smiling tiredly, he began to rub them with the snow. His eyes waited as the color dissolved. His hands were clean. He looked at them and nodded.

"There are no bruises," he murmured. "The blood came from something else."

He paused and watched the snow.

"It is curious," he whispered aloud. "Then I am still mad. Careful . . . mad. For there was blood . . . and not mine. So it would seem I have been seducing myself with optimisms. A true madman. Yes, a lunatic mumbling excitedly to himself in the snow all night, saying:

"Sane. Mallare is quite sane."

He laughed softly.

"Oh, yes. I'm too clever for you, Mallare. Very much too clever. You present a pair of red hands to me. I wash them carefully in the snow. They become white. Interesting phenomena."

He chuckled softly and stared at the snow and swollen trees.

"The old circle again," he murmured. "And I begin the absorbing hide and go seek with my senses. Who am I and where do I end? And who are they and where do they begin? Let us study the phenomenon of red hands. Primo—how do I know there was blood? My eyes said, 'blood.' And the snow is red. But that is only because my eyes, infatuated with an idea, repeat the information.

"But I, Mallare, who am no madman's pawn, no lickspittle secretary to my senses, I say, 'no blood.' I am the Pope. I excommunicate the phenomenon.

"Ah, if there is blood, I fought with one who could bleed. And even my cleverness could not supply arteries in a phantom. Ergo, there is no blood. I am still mad. I see that which is not. But it is nothing to be disturbed about. In fact, it is a diversion."

The snow slowly covered the figure of Mallare. His drawn eyes balanced themselves amid the flakes.

"It snows, snows," he murmured after a pause. "And I remember something. What is it I think! Rita . . . Yes, there would be blood if Rita were . . . Hm, the murdered one. There was something I didn't remember while I walked.

"I can't. Not that way. Careful, Mallare. Be careful. There are thoughts impossible to think. Yes, impossible."

Again silence filled him. His drawn eyes widened.

"Mallare," he whispered, "you are a madman. I know. This chokes. Yes. It was I—I, Mallare. It is I who have been mad. I have been mad myself. Not you. No, not you! But the God—the Strange Pose. I can't. An impossible denouement. My head breaks. Her blood . . . Rita."

He stared open mouthed at a question that circled toward him out of the snow. Words babbled in his head. He shook himself away from them and stared.

"She was alive!" he cried aloud. "My phantom lived. It was I who was the phantom. And she—alive!"

His face whitened, his eyes remained inanimate and gleaming with terror. Then the figure of Mallare fell forward and lay curved in the snow.

[VIII]

ROM *the Journal of Mallare
dated January.*

"I am the one who contemplates. I am the Knowing One. There is nothing I do not know. It is amazing to be Mallare. I have triumphed over five worlds. I look down upon a rabble of Mallares. There are five Mallares—five sullen looking madmen. One of them sits and listens to voices. Another of them wanders about, staring with sad eyes at intolerable visions. Another of them lies on his back, babbling excitedly with the darkness. Another of them eats and sleeps like a prosperous grocer. And there is a fifth Mallare who weeps. A baffling rogue who puts his arms around me and blubbers on my shoulder like a lodge brother. He says nothing, and of them all I dislike him the most.

"His silence is mysterious. His tears are uncomfortable. A distressing ass, weeping, blubbering. He implores me. Aha, I have it. I know his secret. He is memory—a memory of myself following me around like a heartbroken mother a wayward son.

Five Mallares, five sinister comedians to entertain me. And I, what can I call myself—pure reason? No, a disgusting title. Rather, Unreason, since I am after all the Indifferent One. But all this is a quibble inspired by modesty. I am God. I am that which men have worshipped—the aloof one, the pitiless and amused one.

"The five tribes of Mallare rage and curse beneath me, fill the air with profanations, weep and gibber in the night. But I sit inviolate and wait for them—even for that blubbering one whose tongue is thick with tears and whose idiot eyes implore me—and they return. They raise their faces to me, their God, and fall prostrate before my smile.

"Yes, it is the weeping one who causes me the most trouble. A reluctant worshipper who annoys me. He clings like another phantom. A meddlesome imbecile who keeps buttonholing me and pouring out tales of woe. And who keeps my name on his lips. I can see it moving on his lips. But he is dumb. I have his secret though. This dumb one came to me in the snow. I was faint. Hunger had thrown me to the ground. When I stood up he was beside me. His lips moved excitedly but they made no sound. And we walked home together.

"'Who is this pathetic intruder?' I thought. 'He walks beside me gesturing with his lips and weeping, weeping. He falls on my neck and embraces me. His eyes roll with panic. What new variant of madness is this?'

"It is curious that of all the Mallares he alone is speechless. The others keep up their incessant babbling and screaming—true citizens of Bedlam. But this dumb one who attached himself to me in the snow, even his lips have stopped moving now, except to form my name slowly as he blubbers on my shoulder.

"I am kind to him and forgiving. I smile. I even coax him to speak, to move his lips once more. In the snow when he followed me home I was able to detect words his silence spoke.

"'Blood on your hands,' he repeated. 'Think, think, Mallare.'

"I humored him and looked at my hands. They were clean. And I answered him soothingly.

"'You are an interesting quirk,' I said. 'My senses that fancy they have killed a woman have given birth to an illusion of guilt. And you are that illusion. My madness dresses itself in logic like a fishwife hanging rhinestones in her hair.

"'Be calm,' I said, 'Mallare has slain only a phantom, and the murder of illusions is a highly respectable privilege whose exercise is rewarded on earth as well as in heaven.'

"But this creature was not to be diverted from himself.

"'He is another one of them,' I thought. 'He walks and implores and wrings his hand and babbles, 'blood, blood that was real.' And there is nothing to be done with him. Another pathologic symptom asks the hospitality of Mallare, and I must make the proper pretense of graciousness and cordiality.

"'But first I must identify my guest. Take his measure out of the corner of my eye and understand him. Very well, I have been the victim of a hallucination which my senses accepted as real. And which I was able to murder only by pretending I too believed it real. Therefore, having committed this illusory crime, there results this illusory sense of guilt.'

"And thus we walked home, this dumb one and I, his absurd grief confusing me. I will confess. My name on his lips frightened me at first. As it sometimes does now. For he has become more than an illusion of guilt. He is, this sly fellow, a memory, inarticulate and envious. He envies me because I am clever enough to laugh at my madness. However, I will consider him later, in his various guises, for of all the Mallares, dumb though he is and ludicrous with inane tears, he interests me the most.

"We walked home and I finally fell to belaboring him. A pest, a mendicant, a croaking idiot—I cursed him out roundly and refused him further attention. This is the wisest course sometimes. It is dangerous to humor too carelessly these sprawling Mallares. They are slyly at war with my omnipotence. I can understand the anger of God. Sacrilege confuses Him. And We are all alike—We Gods. We are forced into an attitude of indifference in order that We may keep Ourselves intact. Thus We look down with Consummate dispassion upon Our hallucinations—Our worlds. And it is this dispassion that men worship in Us, unable to understand Our lack of interest and terrified by Our aloofness they prostrate themselves before an infinite mystery.

"Yet, though the theology of God has become the secret of My unreason, I find Myself dangerously susceptible. It is when I seek to appease My loneliness by raising one of the babbling ones to My side. He enters My black heaven with a pretense of gratitude, fawning before Me and accepting My fellowship with humility. There follows then a moment of insidious diversion. Slowly a confusion fills Me. Yes, even I am open to confusion. It is a pity I have for the babbling one.

"I listen to his complaints. The sad-eyed Mallare staring at intolerable visions. Mallare, the dark chatterer. Or this other one— My friend the weeping lodge brother. Yes, I pity them and soothe them. But I find Myself singularly moved. Their prayers move Me. They begin to whisper that I return with them. I am tempted to follow them, to let them take My hand and lead Me into their strange houses.

"But I smile in time and My smile, fixed and profound, overcomes them. They prostrate themselves once more before the mystery of My indifference. And I remain the God of Mallare.

"On this day the dumb one sprawled along home with me, there were many curious things happened. I had walked all night in the snow weary with hunger. Rita, who had driven me into a moment of fury—I had destroyed her for the time. A strange destruction during which I pummelled the air like a veritable madman. But the ruse had served to rid me of the hallucination for the night. Finally, tired with walking and hunger, I fell from a bench in the park.

"When I awoke I recalled at once the grotesque struggle of the night. And with this dumb, weeping creature dogging my steps, I returned home. She was still with me. I smiled, although I confess there was despair in my thought. For I had fancied the miserable business of the night had put an end to the hallucination. No, she was still there. She was waiting for me on the couch.

"But my mind had not deceived itself. It was as I had thought. I had planned to rid myself of her by hating this phantom until my hate had darkened it. Then there would be nothing but an imperceptible shadow of her remaining, one with which my senses could no longer seduce themselves.

"And when I came into the room I saw my plot was working. For her eyes no longer gleamed. A radiance had left her.

"'My hate begins to operate upon this chimera,' I thought. I frowned at her and sat down, worn out with the walking of the night.

"'I have undermined the infatuation of this phantom,' I thought. I would have been elate but it occurred to me there was an inconsistency. This dumb one, this sniveling one, persisted. And how should he, who was dependent upon her death for his existence, persist in her presence?' This was a question for Mallare, the indifferent one. This was a query to answer.

"Ah, I will write more about this blubberer, for the answer to him is piquantly involved. It is like a head with too many hats.

But not now—I will not write about him now. I will only bear him in mind.

"She watched me from the couch and I became aware of something. I studied her cautiously. Her eyes no longer gleamed with love. There was a radiance absent.

"'Aha,' I thought, 'she hates. Mallare recovers the strings to his Frankenstein. His puppet dances again to his will. See, my senses no longer leap to her. They tremble warily before the hate in her eyes.'

"I watched her as she watched me. And then an incredible thing happened. She arose from the couch and came slowly toward me and she held a knife in her hand. She came toward me with the knife at her side.

"'Clever,' I thought. 'In fact, a miracle of cleverness. This phantom has gone mad. It is madder than I. It fancies itself able to slay me. It advances upon me with its dagger of mist and it intends to fall upon me. This mysterious logic that grows of itself like a fungus in darkness, where will it end? Already it towers around me—a monstrous weed rising out of my madness, and I am chilled by its shadow.'

"And I continued to think:

" 'I desired to be rid of her. My desire finally overleaped my befuddled senses. And now this desire has become a new soul for my phantom. Yet I planned no details in my desire. I did not will this melodramatic denouement. Then it is obvious that my desire is like a seed filled with hidden life. I blow a thought into my phantom and that thought develops and hatches. This is a phenomenon to be written about.'

"As I thought she came closer and finally stood over me. Her eyes, I observed, were completely mad. Yes, they were like horrible fires. And her face was a marvel of mimicry. The cleverness of my thought appalled me. I said nothing, however, and watched her. She began to talk. I had become used to this phase of the hallucination. But this time my senses shuddered at her words. They who had been so eager to sate themselves in the possession of this chimera and who had betrayed my omnipotence, they now suffered the penalty of their blindness. For it was evident that to them, this chimera was still real. She was an avenger towering with a knife above them.

"But Mallare smiled.

"'See,' he murmured aloud, 'here is the reward of your folly. You would philander with this shadow. You would disport yourself in abominable fornications with this hallucination. Very well, I am amused at your clownish terror even more than I was amused at your burlesque ecstasies. Tremble now for here is a Medusa, a Messilina come to destroy you. Whimper and grovel, but observe in your idiot cowardice how Mallare, the indifferent one, sits and smiles—still supreme, still a spectator ravished by the dark comedy.'

"I could not resist this moment of triumph. I laughed although there was no one to enjoy my laughter. And I watched her. She was still talking, deep, meaningless words. For it was her habit to talk in the gypsy language when moved. Often this fact baffled me. But I perceive now that my thought was a seed containing my omniscience in microcosm. God does not invent languages but He understands them since it is unnecessary for Him to know, in His indifference, what they are saying. And the language my phantom spoke, although foreign to me, was nevertheless an integral part of my thought—another of the manifestations with which God naively astounds Himself. It is His only diversion.

"I was curious concerning the effect upon my senses of this illusory attack. And, I must confess these things simply, there came to me the idea that Mallare might be slain by the cowardice of his senses. There would be nothing illogical in that. For if this chimera had been able to trick them into the illusion of love, it was entirely natural that it should be able to trick them now into the illusion of death. With the exception that death is an illusion even Mallare, the indifferent one, might not survive.

"Ah, Mallare, Mallare! He wanders pensively amid treacherous shadows—Mallare—an image debating subtly the existence of its mirror. I sigh. But it is one of the relaxations of God—to pity Himself His uselessness.

"Her talk came to an end and she raised her knife. Die or not, the thing was too incredible a farce to leave me unmoved. Yes, I laughed out of sheer delight. The drollery of this phantom hacking at Mallare with a non-existent dagger . . . a mad windmill charging Don Quixote! Superb!

"I perceive now a moral in the situation that I did not think of at the time. Sacrilege is a vital danger to God. His omnipotence is dependent upon the submission of His creatures. And they who, inspired with the quaint illusion of their own reality, turn upon Him—ah, they destroy themselves. But their destruction impoverishes their God.

"At the time, however, the spectacle alone and not its significances, preoccupied me. I laughed and reached my hand to the dagger. A sadistic gesture, for I desired to give my senses a taste of its reality and thus enjoy their squirming. Marvelous dagger! The point of it was sharp. Mallare can invent daggers, beautiful daggers that poise melodramatically over his heart, that move slowly in quest of his life's blood! S'death, a property man of parts!

" 'Clever dagger,' I murmured. 'Do you enjoy the illusion of yourself as much as this chimera wielding you quivers with the illusion of impending murder?'

"It paused before me and I nodded. My laughter had halted it. It was evident that my thought operating in this phantom was confused by my laughter. I nodded again.

" 'It would be logical and extremely pleasant,' I thought, 'if this creature, shrinking before the sacrilege of destroying its creator, turned on itself and accomplished a more probable assassination.'

"She stood before me and I was pleased to see her hatred increase. It was amazingly vivid. I observed the viciousness of her features. Her face had become contorted. Its fury was like a mask. But she had dropped the knife. I could not refrain smiling an encouragement at her—the naive applause an author bestows upon his puppets.

"But the plot still contained surprises. Yes astonishing denouements began to crowd the stage. For she started to undress. Here was a trick that baffled Mallare. I winced with distaste.

" 'The consistency which I have hitherto admired in my madness seems rather dubious.' I thought. 'The melodrama of illusions grows too improbable. This fine tragedy crumbles into the ludicrous. She forgets her hate. She is again Rita, the infatuated one. A lightning change that smacks of inferior vaudeville. She is about to undress and resume her deplorable assaults upon my idiot senses. A poorly written business. I have a notion to walk out.'

"But I remained smiling at the absurdity, too tired to leave my chair. I was pleased to notice that her nudity did not this time appeal to my doting madness. This marked an improvement—a foretaste of victory. The disintegration had begun.

"Her body was interesting. It was covered with bruises. There were stains on its flesh. At the sight of them the lodge brother, the sniveling one who had followed me home in the snow, set up a veritable caterwauling. Here was terrible evidence of the fellow's guilt. The bruises of course. An accomplished penitent, this blubberer, able to transform himself from a Sense of Homicidal Guilt into a mere feeling of General Remorse.

"She was not dead. Yet he lingered. And now, at the sight of her bruises, he rushed forward with inferior regrets. He will bear study, this weeping one. Of all the sprawling Mallares, he alone lacks logic. But I will come to him later. The plot is more entertaining than this incongruous spectator weeping and hissing out of turn.

"She began to talk once more and wildly. The sense of it dawned on me. She was calling Goliath. He came shuffling from his usual hiding place—the curtains. A diverting little monster. I bear him no ill will. Although I grow slightly envious of his madness. Yet his madness is a terrific flattery. It is involved and piquant and one of the things that remain for me to study cautiously. The madness of Goliath and, of course, this gentleman Niobe.

"He came out, a fact at the time that astonished me. For I had not been aware of his madness. He stood with his bent and bulbous body shaking and his hands resting like a baboon's on the floor. I was noticing the excitement of his huge head when it came to me with a curious feeling—he was looking at her. Yes, Goliath my servant was looking not at me. But at her!

" 'Careful, Mallare, be careful,' I thought. The insane sniveling of this lodge brother distracted me. His arms came around me and he rested his head on me and wept. Insufferable ass! It was impossible to think. I remained with my eyes watching and repeating cautiously to myself the warning.

"Here was a trick too baffling for Mallare. Mallare must suspend himself, close his eyes and climb slowly back into his black heaven.

" 'Then Goliath too is a phantom,' I thought. 'But careful, be careful, Mallare. That is too easy. And you remember. It is dangerous to hide from too many memories. They will become shadows that nibble at you. He is not a phantom. Goliath is no chimera. He lives. He has reality.

" 'Then how does it come,' I continued thinking, 'that he sees that which is visible only to you? His eyes are fastened on her who is to be seen only inside the caverns of Mallare. He raises his arms. His hands touch her. I am imagining Goliath. Goliath is not in the room. This is a memory of him that has wandered onto the scene of my madness.'

"Here my thinking ended. I sat contemplating the imbecile, the blubberer. He pressed himslf upon me with his shameless importunings. He snivelled and his lips moved with my name. I watched them say, 'Mallare' and repeat 'Mallare' till I grew dizzy with the pantomime of my name. I will study this later and discover the secret of his lips. My name drifting continually over them has a way of hypnotizing me. But later—later.

"I began thinking once more.

" 'This lodge brother weeps while Goliath takes liberties with my phantom. There is a connection there. But it is unimportant for the present. I must discover something else.'

"Then, like a victory too long withheld, it came to me. He was mad. Goliath, my servant, was mad. But more than that—a telepathic madness. I have elaborated my understanding since. Goliath suffers from a contagion. His constant attendance upon me has proved fatal to his stupidity. His senses are the victims of my puppets. He has entered my world and my madness creates for him, as it does for me, shadows that deceive him. But there is no Mallare in him. Unlike me, he does not sit in amused judgment upon himself.

"It is an interesting phenomenon—this strange mesmerism. It remains to be studied. Goliath and I are mad brothers. This understanding arrived in time. Or else I would have flung myself in despair upon the ever-imploring bosom of my lugubrious sniveler.

"Rita was real to Goliath. I watched him excitedly and continued to think. I addressed myself:

"'Observe,' I said, 'here you have a distressing visualization. Goliath, your dwarf, mimics your madness. And it is not pleasant to look at. His eyes roll with passion. His fat lips chew upon lewd expectations. His fingers raise themselves like frightened blasphemies to her breasts. And he watches you. Yes, his eyes sneak glimpses of you. For you are his rival! You and this nigger monster are vaginal comrades. It is pleasant to see that you have the decency to feel enraged. Five infatuated Mallares sputtered and wept and gnashed their teeth.

"As I talked I turned my attention to her. In my excitement over Goliath I had ignored

her. Her hands were fumbling with the clothes
of this doting rival. But her eyes were on me.
They blazed.

"'This pantomime of shadows grows
involved,' I thought. But I was experimenting
with rhetoric. For the thing was absurdly simple. Hate still animated my phantom. And
this was her revenge. She was about to give
herself to the black dwarf Goliath. She was
about to commit sexual hari-kari.

"I watched her hands remove his clothes,
his red jacket, his fine shirt. He jumped up
and down like a distracted child, his own hands
bewildered with too many activities. They fondled her, they tugged at his trousers. They
became insane and flapped at his sides. She
helped him, her eyes still watching me.

"'At last I produce a horror worthy of
myself,' I thought. 'The mist dagger was melodrama to be smiled at. But this—ah, here we
have a refinement that reduces death to a minor
obscenity. She attacks me now with a weapon
worthy my indifference. It is true, my senses

writhe less frightenedly. But I, Mallare—yes, Mallare the Supreme One—honor her assault with a shudder.

" 'Ah, who but Mallare could have invented so subtle a blasphemy, so accomplished an enemy. It is an old theological quibble, but I understand it now. God is the greatest atheist. He is proud of a disbelief in Himself.

" 'Yes, this phantom is the atheism of Mallare. And it is at last a true child. A parental pride excites me. Like Mallare, her father, she rises above herself. I have breathed the soul of hate into her. My hatred alive with a cleverness of its own speaks to itself.

" 'It says, 'I am the hatred of Mallare. I desire to murder him. I am his phantom, but the suffering and insult he has heaped upon me grow unbearable. His cruelty and coldness have filled me with fury. I would have killed him but that would have been almost an infidelity. For his senses have been my lovers. I remember them with tears. I decided not to kill him because that would have meant to kill his senses. But this other one, this Insufferable and Aloof One—this Serene One staring amusedly at me out of His black heaven—how send my hatred against him? Ah, I will conspire with his senses. I am no more than an idea in the head of God. But the head of God is but an idea that encircles me. I am a phantom within a phantom. Thus I must make myself nauseous. I must make myself too hideous. I must make myself so monstrous that the Idea which contains me will feel an anguish. And this anguish will be the applause to my hate.'

"I sat shrewdly silent, for the moment was approaching. At last I perceived myself behind the logic of this Frankenstein. For it was I—I, Mallare—that was attacking myself with this hatred. It was Mallare who was arranging this little plot for himself. And why? Because then the head of Mallare, nauseated by the vileness of the assault, would disgorge forever the hallucination of Rita. It was an emetic Mallare had found necessary to administer to himself.

"Ah, my cleverness grows incredible. I am too Supreme to grasp Myself. There are still unexplored crevices in My infinity, and out of these continue to issue surprises that divert Me.

"Goliath was undressed. His black body, lumped and like some mad caricature of itself, gleamed in the light.

"'See,' I said. 'Note this bulbous little black man. For he is a caricature not of himself but of you. He is a rival before whom your senses wince as before some unflattering image. Yes—the image of Mallare stands saluting his charming chimera with an interesting Ethiopian erection. For though they differ in many externals, Mallare and Goliath are one. They are ornamented insulations for an identical current. And here, throbbing under an erection is the current of Mallare and of an infinity of Mallares.

"'Ah, the penis of this dwarf is repellent because that which Mallare so fondly called his own—his desires—is revealed to him as grotesquely promiscuous. Yes, the penis is the democratic tabernacle of Life. Under its little Moorish roof, the senses of the race kneel in common prayer.

" 'Observe it, Mallare. It is the rendez-vous of expiring illusions, the gathering place of the anonymities which utilize man, beasts and plants. See how this curious dwarf staggers like a bewildered stranger in its shadow. He is an outcast. He is useless. He is no longer necessary. Life which made a pretense of him, enters its tabernacle and closes the doors on him. Here is the great secret. Here stands the grim tyrant before whose delicious wrath man bows himself into annihilations.

" 'Ah, what a marvelous tabernacle! It moves and Goliath follows. It points and Goliath runs after it. An infatuated tabernacle that fancies itself going to Heaven! It is proud. It struts. Goliath shuffles after it like a forlorn little nigger in the wake of a circus. It leaps. And Goliath gallops after it. Aha! he lies on his back impaled. But she!'

"They were on the couch. She sat beside him but her eyes still sought me. Noises issued from Goliath. He rolled on his back, kicking crooked legs and yelping.

"I watched her white body spread over him. Her eyes left me and my rhetoric dwindled into a sigh. I was alone with a spectacle. Goliath masturbating with a phantom—but not as Mallare had done. No, not as Mallare who had lain indifferent beside his Frankenstein. For Goliath's arms were around her, his legs entwined her. His body, an insanity in itself, made a mate beneath her more incredible than she. There was silence. Then she screamed!——

"Yes, Mallare closed his eyes. A coldness tiptoed out of his heart. She was laughing. Her laughter entered his ears—a noise that was like a witch's flight of sound. But who was it laughed? Mallare, Mallare laughed. It was his voice in the phantom that laughed at him. It was his hallucination he had loved that now gave itself to a little monster. And it was his hate that designed this laugh, a thing that pierced the heaven in which he sat. Mallare closed his eyes, a God shuddering before His own atheism. Yes, rhetoric now. It is easy to write. My words embroider themselves.

"But then, when the laugh struck Mallare! Ah, there was curious mutiny. They went away. The little Mallares who worship me went away, all but one. The dumb one. Yes, I write of him again. He came to me then and his tears were more horrible than the scream I had heard. His weeping came too close. His weeping grew too loud. His arms embraced me and he held his face too close to mine. And my name rose from his lips.

"I was alone with him and my fingers fought with his throat. This blubberer who had followed me home in the snow, yes this insufferable melancholiac who rained his tears into my Heaven—Mallare would have killed him.

"But he was too sly. He slipped away and sprawled around the room. He beat his hands against walls and tore at his hair. I followed watching him and coaxing him to come close once more. I smiled at him to come near again. But no, he avoided me. He stood against the curtains facing me and pointing his finger at me. His mouth was open but no sound came from it. There was only the noise of my phantom laughing.

"He stood pointing and I watched my name come like a dead shout from his lip. His throat was alive with my name.

" 'Mallare!' it said.

"I smiled at him. And I worshipped aloud so that he might hear. I whispered to him to come close—this lugubrious blasphemer who wears my name in his throat. But his face grew white. His arms dropped and he leaned against the curtains. His eyes closed and he fell. The Indifferent One remained. The smile of Mallare remained contemplating the prostrate ones.

"The couch was still alive. But it was dark. Her outline was already disintegrating. Goliath's fingers stared from her back.

" 'The dark comedy ends,' I thought. 'My phantom dissolves in a suicidal orgasm. And the little monster beneath her collapses amid too sudden memories. Finis! The revenge that I so cleverly manipulated is accomplished. And now Mallare disgorges a hallucination become too nauseous. I have fouled this pretty one so that my senses might abandon her. And see, they whimper under me. The dumb one lies in a corner and even his tears are ended. And this sad eyed one, weary with intolerable visions, and this one whose ears are filled with voices—all of them whimper under me. But I must feel no pity for them. Mallare rides away like a star. . . .

" 'And she dissolves. Vale Rita! The red and yellow dress again. Yes . . . yes—the green and orange shawl again. Put them on. Bravo Rita! Tragedy bows in a decorative anti-climax. Little one, Mallare banishes thee from His heaven where thou becamest too intimate. Because thou sought to seduce His worshippers. Vale!—Mallare disgorges thee. Spit not at Me, little one, for I am only a smile. Spit at this dumb one, this blubberer, who has forgotten himself in a new sleep.'

* * * * *

"And Goliath weeps. She is gone and his madness regrets her vanishing. He sits by day and watches out of the window. At night I have found him staring at the couch where he lay with my shadow. He kneels beside it with his grotesque arms flung out, embracing memories.

"His madness flatters me. Yet it is a thing to be studied. His eyes are insane. They roll continually in their sockets. He beats himself, knocking his fists against his head. And I have discovered him on the floor doubled up, his head buried in his arms. He does not hear me but remains, while I move around, immobile as an idol. Yes, little Goliath is mad. But he cannot recover the illusion whose memory haunts his dark soul. He suffers. He beats his head and his tears are futile. For she was mine. Mallare created her. Mallare destroyed her. There is a temptation at times to return her—

not to Mallare but to this poor dwarf who expires under his grief.

"I am tempted by his madness. Goliath has found no God in his black heaven. I would be his God and create for him as I may for Myself. But I am wary of such altruism. He is still My servant and looks after Me. But My smile watches him with caution. His eyes roll too much.

"Since I rid myself of her, there has been no mutiny. I sit and contemplate problems that have grown too simple for me. And when I am bored with studying Goliath's madness, I divert myself with my friend, the lodge brother. A baffling imbecile who withholds himself slyly. I have not yet come to an understanding with him. There are too few facts to go on. He is silent. He weeps. My name sleeps forever on his lips. And once he babbled to me of blood on my hands. These are the only realities that form a key to him.

"His presence remains a discomfort. We sit and stare at each other. And I talk quietly to him.

" 'You are an inconsistent ass,' I say. 'You were first an obvious pathologic symptom—an illusory conscience born to adorn the grief of my senses that fancied they had murdered Rita, the phantom. But then when you found her alive, what did you do? Did you vanish as, in all logic, you should? For Rita was not murdered and therefore where the necessity of a conscience to celebrate her crime?

" 'But you remained and grew more dolorous. Then you are something else. I suspect you of being the adroit ambassador the madmen have sent into my heaven to plead their cause. Yet why do you not plead? As an ambassador you are a tongue-tied, sniveling idiot. Therefore again, you escape logic. And without logic my madness becomes slyly incomprehensible to me.

" 'We watch each other like two careful wrestlers, eh? But what hold do you want? Tell me and I will let you try your strength. No—tears, nothing else. You weep, weep until the sight of you is an impossible ennui.

"'Ah, perhaps you are a memory of Mallare. Something forgotten. Logic approaches you as I think. Something forgotten. And you are overcome at my infidelity. Like Goliath you mourn a vanished one. But there is this difference. Whereas Goliath is real and the object of his mourning is a phantom—you and not I are the phantom. Yes, a phantom mourns me. But speak then. I have no objection to memory. Let me hear what this is all about and I will admit what you say. I will admit it all beforehand.

"'But no. You expect something else. You expect Mallare to fall at your feet and embrace you. I can see that in your eyes—a monotonous expectation that grows ludicrous. Yes, your tears grow ludicrous. I tolerate you for only one purpose. You are a problem that diverts me. For if I desired I could do with you as I did with Rita. There are ways to make you too nauseous.

"'Yes, I might invent another hate for myself. My hands might tear you as they tore her. And then, filled with a fury against me, you too might turn to Goliath. He is still mad, my dwarf, and susceptible to the phantoms I send him. Do you want to go to him as she did? Aha! You wince. Remember then that Mallare has it in his power to send you to his dwarf, to make you take her place over his terrible body. And Mallare will do this if you annoy him too much. And then, sickened with you as he was with her, he will disgorge another shadow. Let us be frank about this. I warn you.'

"Thus I sit and talk quietly to this weeping one. And when I stop I watch his lips move with my name.

"'Mallare,' they say.

"This is his only answer to my overtures. But I will win him over. He will come close to my smile and kneel finally before me. He will confess who he is and what my name means.

"I grow tired. Goliath stands by his shrine and weeps. He waits beside a couch as if it were another Mallare able to give birth to a phantom. Poor dwarf, unlike Mallare he has not learned that suffering is an illusion, that couches and Medusas are illusions. Unlike Mallare there is no smile hanging its star above him.

"Sleep comes. A forgotten world babbles with shadows outside my windows. It is time to say goodnight to my friend, the lodge brother. Turn your tears to the cold moon, my friend. Mallare goes away. Far away into a house where he is alone."

{IX}

HE last entry in the Journal of Mallare—undated.

"Talk to me, Mallare. Tell me. Where am I? He grows larger, this dumb one. He moves away, growing larger. He defies distance. He grows too large to see. But his tears remain.

"Whisper to me, Mallare. He vanishes and I must sneak after him. Call me back. He is strange. His darkness lures me out of my heaven. A little whisper will save me. You will say to me, 'Here is God.' I will come back.

"My words tire of him. He will not listen. His tears! dear God, are You so human that they silence You? He has come into my loneliness. And there is no use debating with him any longer. Since he followed me home in the snow his weeping has never wavered. I must talk not to him but to Mallare. I must debate with Mallare. But where is he, this Supreme One? Mallare, where art thou?

"Yes, my madness becomes an increasing novelty. I remain. But I grow smaller. I am too small. Where is my smile? It hides from me. But his tears fall. This dumb one knows how to weep. Alas, I drown.

"Come to my side. I will whisper. I am in love. Yes, do not be astonished. I am in love with her. You recall her? She was like a curtain fluttering before the door of enchantments. Her breasts were like little blind faces raised in prayer. Yes, Rita, my radiant one. The phantom I constructed. The Phoenix that arose in my soul. And that I slew again. I am in love. But my magic no longer works. She does not return.

"I will whisper. I kneel with Goliath beside the couch. Ah, Mallare, Mallare—I am mad with love. I weep and beat my head. And this other one calls me away. His shape grows larger and his darkness lifts me toward it. He pulls me from the couch. Talk to me, Mallare. I am mad, but talk to me and I will understand. Dear, shining Mallare . . . Tell me 'no' and I will break my love. I will put my fist through the window out of which I watch for her. And it will be finished.

"But I weep. My eyes have caught his trick. I weep for her. Do you understand this? My beautiful one whom I disgorged. Yes, Rita. I die with love of her. I kneel by the bed that knew her. Whisper back to me, Mallare, that I am mad. And I will laugh. But without you I grow too small to laugh.

"There is pain in the shadows. I ask, where am I? Go way, then, Mallare. Leave me. I persist without Mallare. I remain. Let me dissolve into this. Let me sprawl before the door of enchantments. It is illusion. Let it be. She will come out. Rita, my vanished one, come back to me. It is I who ask. Not the Cold One, not the Indifferent One, not Mallare. But I . . . I.

"I will hold you in my arms. I will feed your mist with kisses. My body will warm you. I will be kind. I am not Mallare. He is gone. He hides. He will not come back. I will kneel before the door that sings with you. I am mad with love. See, Rita, I am like Goliath. My eyes roll. I am mad and you may come to me without fear.

"Windows break in me again. I remember this from long ago. Hey, you blubbering one! Do you want me! Hey, you brother sniveler, come back! I laugh. Do you understand this? A laughter without definitions. Ah, forgive me. You sat and wept and I scolded. Come back and sit again. I will fall at your feet. Your eyes asked that. But now—where are your feet? There is no shape. How am I to know where? Come back. Here, sit in this chair beside me. God! In silence, I utter my name. But it is a name that has flown away, flown away.

"Hey, you, bring me my name. The little name, the one that made a pantomime on your lips. The one that stared at me with letters. Bring me my name, I will understand its meaning. My other name has flown away. Listen. Let me whisper. Bring it to me and I will place it like a gate before the door of enchantments. I will kneel to it. Windows break in my head. Mallare . . . are you Mallare? No, you are this. You are a babble of words that stands on its nose.

"Laugh at me, Mallare. Let me hear your laugh far away. Or I go. Listen, Mallare. I turn my back on this darkness. I do not kneel at empty couches. No. I wait for you. You were my God. You, the One who contemplated. Yes, my arms are out to You. Come . . . a whisper out of silences. Hey, Mallare. I dissolve. I become a little phantom. A useless little phantom. I drift like Rita. And they attack me. Hands, voices and trembling ones. They are brave because it is dark. Your wor-

shippers, Mallare, they turn on me. They break
windows. Pity me. This is the cross.

אלי, אלי למה עזבתני